HOW TO SAVE A UNICORN

Books by Meg Cannistra
available from Inkyard Press

How to Heal a Gryphon
How to Save a Unicorn

HOW TO SAVE A UNICORN

MEG CANNISTRA

ISBN-13: 978-1-335-45802-5

How to Save a Unicorn

Copyright © 2023 by Cake Creative LLC

In association with

For questions and comments about the quality of this book, please contact us
at CustomerService@Harlequin.com.   NOV - - 2023

Inkyard Press
22 Adelaide St. West, 41st Floor
Toronto, Ontario M5H 4E3, Canada
www.InkyardPress.com

Printed in U.S.A.

For my husband, Dan, who showed me magic
can be found everywhere—even at Teterboro Airport.

1

Every morning at around seven o'clock, Mrs. and Mr. Calamoneri greet the day with song. Sometimes it's Mrs. Calamoneri's favorite, Erykah Badu, other times it's Mr. Calamoneri's Frank Sinatra playlist coming from the speakers. But I like it best when they sing with each other. The sounds of sausages sizzling and eggs frying are the backing track to their expert harmonizing. Their breakfast performance drifts under my door, dancing around my room and mingling with the tempting scents of maple and butter. Even if their magic didn't manifest through music, it would still be one of the most beautiful songs I've ever heard.

And then there's me: I sound like Sinistro coughing up a hair ball when I try to carry a tune.

"Took you long enough," the cat in question says as he slinks back and forth in front of my dresser.

I toss my pillow at Sinistro, missing him by several feet, before throwing the duvet back and swinging my legs over the side of my bed. Mornings and I will never get along but waking up to a full breakfast and the Calamoneris singing beats Rocco banging on my door to rush me off to guaritore school without so much as a piece of toast.

The faint twisting of homesickness knots in my belly and I touch the cornicello hanging from my neck. On my nightstand is a picture of Mamma, Papa, Rocco, Zia Clementina, Sinistro, and me inside the Colosseum. We went just before I flew here, to New Jersey. My apprenticeship was technically supposed to start on January 1, but I didn't have to leave until February to give us some time to recover from the Great Kidnapping (my parents, zia, Rocco, and Alessia were all held captive by the Streghe del Malocchio last year). It was nice spending time together and sightseeing without having to hide my secret from them—that I don't belong in guaritore school, because I'm not a guaritrice. That I'm not a healer of humans like them, and that I never will be. To finally be accepted as a follower of Diana, goddess of wild animals—and to get to spend my time learning to care for creatures, ordinary and extraordinary!

The homesickness floats away, disappearing at the thought. Even if Papa is still a *teensy* bit nervous about it all, he's come a long way in respecting my goals. And Zia Clementina's, too. They argue on occasion, but it lacks the anger they once clung to. Now they bicker just like Rocco and me.

I hop out of bed and change into a red denim skirt, pink sweater, and white tights dotted with red and pink hearts. I plop my hair into a bun on the top of my head and grab my vet's log off my desk.

"Now who's the slowpoke?" I grin and open the door as Sinistro grooms his long black fur.

"Oh, hush. *I'm* not the one who has training in an hour." He stretches, his whiskers twitching, before sauntering out into the hall.

"But you gotta come with me." I follow him down the stairs, the singing growing louder as we pass through the foyer and into the open living room that leads into the kitchen. Now it's only Mrs. Calamoneri's voice I hear as she sings "Love Like This" by Faith Evans—a singer she introduced me to within the first week of living with them. Mrs. Calamoneri's love for female R & B singers is already growing on me.

Mrs. Calamoneri stands at the stove, piling the sausages onto a plate. She's already done her makeup for the day, but the freckles on her face are still visible under her foundation and the pink blush she's wearing highlights the warm undertones in her brown skin. Her eyes are light brown and shine in the sunlight filtering through the windows. A floral headband keeps her curly black hair off her face and she's got on navy dress slacks and a matching blazer.

She turns and greets us with a smile. "Good morning, good morning, Giada and Sinistro." Even when not singing, Mrs. Calamoneri's voice carries a lilt that envelops you in a warm hug.

She's a strega—known as a witch in America—but not a guaritrice. With her magic, she creates wonderful things for people to enjoy. She doesn't honor any god or goddess, but rather honors humanity with her art. And her art is song. Opera, to be specific. It's spellbinding, the way she channels her magic into all sorts of beauty. With her voice alone, she can bring people peace and calm. Or inspire them to go after their goals. Or persuade them to find love. She's one of the most famous opera singers in America and is now making a name for herself all over the world. People line up to hear her, to be awed and moved by her song. It's an incredible and rare gift. One that, if in the wrong hands, could be dangerous. But Mrs. Calamoneri would never use her power to hurt people. All she wants to do is share the happiness she feels every day.

"Buon giorno." I wander over to the fridge to get the glass container of the special cat food I prep for Sinistro every week and scoop a half cup of it into his dish. He twists between my legs, purring as he launches himself at his breakfast.

"Someone's hungry this morning," Mrs. Calamoneri says, laughing.

I hoist myself onto a barstool at the kitchen island and say, "Someone's *always* hungry."

"Sinistro and I have that in common." Mrs. Calamoneri sets a plate of sausage, eggs, and fruit in front of me. Before digging in, I drizzle the sausage and eggs in hot sauce. Nothing's better than hot sauce on fried eggs. I poke one of my sausages in the runny egg yolk and delight in the spicy, salty, peppery flavor as it hits my tongue. One of the things I like best about the Calamoneris is they love to eat, just like me. And they never judge me if I go back for more food. My family doesn't either, but some people can be nosy about that. Which is totally ridiculous if you ask me. People need to mind their own business.

Mrs. Calamoneri asks the speaker on the countertop to play *Cheek to Cheek*, the album by Lady Gaga and Tony

Bennett. The first time they played the album for me, Mr. Calamoneri gasped when I told him I didn't know who Tony Bennett was (but that I loved Lady Gaga). Mrs. Calamoneri had to remind him that I was only thirteen and not from a musical family.

"Giada! Good morning!" Mr. Calamoneri calls as he steps in from the garage. His voice is deep and also has a smooth, musical quality to it—as if he were born to be a crooner. He hangs his coat on the hook by the door and runs a hand through his fluffy brown-and-silver hair. His white skin is flushed pink from the cool early spring morning. He grins and his dark brown eyes crinkle, his bushy brown eyebrows scrunching. Like Mrs. Calamoneri, he's also dressed for the day, in a white button-down and pair of gray slacks.

Mr. Calamoneri is a guaritore, like my parents and brother, but his methods are nontraditional. Rather than focus on potions and regular spellcasting to heal people, he weaves spells and charms into music. It's definitely not the way things are done back in Italy, but I've seen Mr. Calamoneri's musical magic therapy in action and it works. Just last week he taught a woman who had a never-ending case of bronchitis a song-spell that soothed her throat and made it so she could eat solid food again.

"I missed you, babe!" He walks over to Mrs. Calamoneri and plants a kiss right on her cheek.

She swats at him, laughing. "You were gone for less than five minutes taking out the trash."

"Still. Five minutes away from you may as well be a lifetime."

"You're so dramatic." Mrs. Calamoneri rolls her eyes but can't keep the smile from her lips.

Mr. Calamoneri grins at her as he picks up the latest copy of "Magic Makes Perfect"—the newsletter devoted to all things fixer related—and settles onto the barstool next to mine.

My phone buzzes and I pull it out of my pocket. It's a text from Alessia—my best friend who is also doing her apprenticeship in America. She's asking me to call her, but I don't have time this morning—gotta finish eating and get to work!

Alessia's spending the year with the Pulaskis. They run a unicorn sanctuary just outside of Chicago where they focus on rehabilitation and education. Alessia was paired with the Pulaskis because of her desire to specialize in soul healing, which unicorns are vital for. It's a huge deal that she's learning more about soul healing—it's not something most guaritori, especially those that are only thirteen, get to do. And she gets to train in a place where she'll learn so much.

Mrs. Calamoneri places a plate in front of Mr. Calamoneri and another filled with freshly scrambled eggs and a side of melon at an empty spot before walking over to the stairs and calling, "Moss! Your breakfast's going to get cold if you don't hurry up."

"Hang on!" Moss yells back.

Coo. Coo. Coooo. A familiar song trills from the living room swiftly followed by the sound of wings gliding through the air. Fe, Moss's familiar, flies into the kitchen and alights on the fridge. She preens, her beautiful white feathers gleaming in the sunlight.

Much to the surprise, and happiness, of his parents, Moss found out he wasn't a guaritore like his dad, but rather a magical vet. Like me. Moss was surprised, too. He hadn't felt the calling like I had. Instead, he kind of fell into it face-first. Almost literally: he was riding his skateboard and swerved out of the way of an injured Fe. He nursed her back to health with ease and then she started talking to him just like Sinistro talked to me. Mr. Calamoneri once told me that Moss used to be at the top of his class—he always had his nose in a spell book and could often be found practicing different kinds of magic to help animals—but I haven't seen that in the two months that

I've been here. And most of the time I find that version of Moss hard to even imagine anymore. Back when we were pen pals, writing letters and sometimes talking on the phone, Moss tended to be a bit of a know-it-all about magic and his schoolwork. He got to specialize at his school because he met Fe when he was ten, and so he has had *three years* of magical vet classes. I, on the other hand, wasted so much of my time in guaritore school listening to teachers like Maestra Vita drone on and on about things I didn't care about. But despite those head starts, there are reasons why he's now falling behind.

Today feels like one of those days Moss would rather be anywhere but here as the joy in the kitchen is replaced with his grumpy energy. He tromps down the stairs, passes through the living room, and slouches onto the barstool next to his dad's. He's still in his pajamas, wearing a pair of black sweatpants and a navy blue T-shirt with the NASA logo on it. Like his mom, Moss has freckles that cover his light brown face, mainly across the bridge of his nose. His eyes are the same color as his mom's, but he has his dad's bushy eyebrows.

Moss looks tired—more so than usual. He buries a hand in his thick black curls and his shoulders slump forward. Fe hops from the fridge and lands in front of his plate. She nudges her head against his hand, and he gives her a pat.

Moss picks at his eggs, cutting them up with his fork but never actually eating any.

Mr. Calamoneri glances at his son from the corner of his eye and says, "Hmm. There's an article in here about a magical mechanic in Berlin working on fuel alternatives by experimenting with different spells and potions. She's presenting her findings at the magical mechanics summit next month in London."

Moss doesn't look up from his plate.

"I need to head into the city for a rehearsal. Moss, are you and Fe going to join in on the house calls today?" Mrs. Calamoneri asks, her voice laced with hope as she pours coffee into a thermos.

He shrugs. "I don't feel like it."

Mrs. Calamoneri stares at him for a moment before eating some eggs off Mr. Calamoneri's plate.

Mr. Calamoneri nudges Moss. "C'mon. You can't let Gi and Sinistro have all the fun."

"What if Sinistro tries to eat Fe?" Moss asks, eyeing Sinistro. "That cat looks pretty hungry."

"Sinistro doesn't like feathers," I sniff, petting Sinistro's back. "Besides, he's a very good boy."

"Yeah, yeah, yeah," Moss says and forces down a piece of cantaloupe. "You never know with cats."

I know he's just in a mood. I've seen Moss cuddle up

with Sinistro and shower him with belly rubs. Still. It's annoying when he's such a grump. But it's not his fault he doesn't feel well. It's his Crohn's.

"I'm gonna go back to bed. I don't think I can stomach another breakfast of scrambled eggs and cantaloupe." Moss hops down from the stool and Fe jumps onto his shoulder.

"I could make you some oatmeal," Mrs. Calamoneri says.

"I'm just tired of all these boring foods." Moss grimaces and passes into the living room. "All I want is a Taylor ham, egg, and cheese on a toasted everything bagel with extra sriracha. That's my favorite breakfast. But cheese makes me feel iffy now. Eating's like a chore."

"Do you want me to call Dr. Caruso?"

"I don't need extra therapy. We don't talk about anything anyway." He shrugs. "The breathing exercises help some, but other than that…"

"Moss—" Mrs. Calamoneri begins, but Moss sighs.

"Have a good time with the house calls. I promise I'll do my reading and take notes," he says before one of his parents can ask.

Moss started feeling off in his final semester. He'd go to his friends' houses to eat pizza and play video games, but then end up in the bathroom the rest of the night. After completing his schooling, he began his apprenticeship with a magical vet in Queens but had to pause it after only a couple weeks because he was feeling worse than he'd ever felt before and had to go to the hospital. It was a month later—a little after I arrived—that his doctor diagnosed him with Crohn's. The sharp stomach pains, fevers, weight loss—it all added up. While it's been good for him to have a diagnosis after being sick and confused for so long, finding the right treatment has been a challenge.

Mr. Calamoneri's magic has helped, but only a little. And, even before his official diagnosis, he's been in therapy to help find ways to cope with the uncertainty and physical discomfort. His doctors say it can be a learning curve, adjusting to living in a body that operates differently than how it used to. Moss has been understandably frustrated. Not to mention, feeling so down and all the cramping and exhaustion can make it hard for him to access his magic. Sometimes Moss comes with Mr. Calamoneri and me on house calls so he can continue training, but usually he's more comfortable studying from home with Fe.

"Gi and I will fill you in. Go get some rest. I love you, son," Mr. Calamoneri says.

"I know." And Moss trudges back upstairs, in and out of the kitchen in all of fifteen minutes.

Mrs. and Mr. Calamoneri exchange a look. "I'll call Dr.

O'Shea on the way to rehearsal. Maybe we can get him in by the end of the week."

"I should be able to help him more." Mr. Calamoneri shakes his head. "My magic barely makes a dent in his symptoms."

"You've helped, Leo. Just give it some time. It's not about curing his symptoms, but learning to live—and live well—*with* them." Mrs. Calamoneri packs up her bag, kisses Mr. Calamoneri, and crouches down to scratch behind Sinistro's ears. "I should be back by four o'clock today." She stares between us, grinning. "Have a good day, you two."

With that, Mrs. Calamoneri leaves, her heels clicking across the hardwood floors.

Mr. Calamoneri turns to me, his lips quirking upward. "Are you ready? Big day today."

I hop off the barstool and make my way into the living room where I left my backpack. Over my shoulder, I say, "Of course I'm ready."

"Good, good. Who's on our list of house calls this morning?"

I fish my vet's log out of my bag's front pocket and flip to the last page where I hastily scrawled down the three appointments we have today. "First up is Mrs. Donoghue. Her sons are afflicted with some kind of sickness that's caused them to feud endlessly. You prescribed Buon Sangue and we're checking on their progress."

"Very good. Who's after them?" Mr. Calamoneri walks the breakfast plates over to the sink and scrubs them clean.

I scan my list and say, "James and Tim Richardson. James was diagnosed with tinnitus after a bad case of bronchitis. We're checking him out for the first time today to see what treatment options he has."

"Ah, yes." Mr. Calamoneri wipes down the dishes and puts them back in the cabinet. "Should be simple. Who else do we have today?"

"Umm…" I turn the page, trying to find the last name among my doodles of turtles and jackalopes. "Ah! Here we go. Lula Garcia has a frog in her throat. It's been tangled in her vocal cords, and she's lost her voice. She's a new patient and her dad was referred to you by the Moya family. You said music, something like humming, should coax the frog from her throat and help her speak again."

"Classic case." Mr. Calamoneri pours the rest of the coffee in his own travel mug and packs his leather doctor's bag. "Sounds like a jam-packed day. Ready to go?"

I look down at Sinistro and snatch up my backpack. "Always!"

2

"You're doing great so far, Lula." Mr. Calamoneri finishes washing his hands at the Garcias' kitchen sink. Lula sits on a kitchen chair, her mamma and papa on either side. Her mamma's green eyes are wide with alarm, and she keeps running her brown hands through her long, wavy brown hair. Her papa's just as nervous as he rubs at the black scruffy beard on his brown face and fidgets with his silver cufflinks. Lula's a couple years younger than me with big hazel eyes and wavy brown hair that hangs from her head like curtains. She's wearing pink-and-green-polka-dot pajamas and a blue bathrobe. Her brown skin's pale, almost green. Most likely from being sick. I watch them from the other side of the table, furiously scribbling down notes as Mr. Calamoneri talks. Sometimes I get distracted during our house calls because they tend to be pretty boring—like the ones I used to go on with Rocco. (Those were always just boring human stuff, like making elixirs for earaches or spells to ward off night terrors.) But this one's interesting. A frog in the throat's unusual. And if a frog's stuck in a throat, it'll likely need my help once it gets out.

Mr. Calamoneri sits down opposite Lula, puts on a pair of gold spectacles, and continues, "Judging from the scale exercise we just did I'd say that frog is stuck deep down. I'll need to see in your throat now. Please open your mouth wide and say *ahhh*."

Lula tries to follow Mr. Calamoneri's instructions, but only the tiniest squeak comes out. Mr. Calamoneri leans forward and shines a light into her mouth. He adjusts his spectacles and squints into her mouth.

Ribbet.

"Was that what I think it was?" Sinistro asks from his spot on the kitchen chair next to mine.

Lula clamps her mouth shut and looks up at her mamma.

"Oh, it's only gotten worse," Mrs. Garcia cries. She runs her hand through Lula's hair and shakes her head. "How could this even happen?"

"A frog in the throat happens a few ways." Mr. Calamoneri stands and begins setting up the keyboard he brings along to every house call. It's rickety and outdated, its legs attached with duct tape. But it's full of magic, like the cornicelli we wear for protection or any other kind of talisman. Mr. Calamoneri says he's had it since he was thirteen and took his guaritore oath.

He continues, "Swimming in fresh water during a waxing moon, talking too loud, sleeping with your mouth open." Mr. Calamoneri flips the switch on the keyboard and runs his fingers over the keys in a tune that electrifies the magic on my skin. "That last one's especially dangerous. You'd be surprised how many critters wriggle their way into your mouth at night."

"Ew, really?" Mr. Garcia asks. "Remind me never to sleep again."

Mr. Calamoneri shrugs. "Fortunately, it's not dangerous unless it goes on for too long. Lucky for us, we've caught this little fella at just the right time."

Mr. Calamoneri turns to me and says, "Gi, will you please prep the terrarium?"

I open my backpack and start pulling out a variety of jars and crocks. To my left is a small terrarium we picked up on the way to the Garcias'. When Mr. Calamoneri warned that extracting the frogs often led to their deaths, I told him that wouldn't be happening on my watch and asked him to stop by a pet store for a comfortable place for the frog to live while I nurse it back to health.

"Do you have everything you need?" Sinistro places his front paws on the table and takes a closer look at my supplies. The Garcias look at me oddly, but it's only because other people see Sinistro and me as meowing to each other when we talk.

"I hope so. I have immortal jellyfish goo, which'll help heal any wounds it might have." I open the lid on a small silver crock and then grab a glass jar filled with murky water. "And some water from Lake Nemi, blessed by Diana. Obviously. Fresh water's essential for amphibians." I rattle a plastic container and add, "I also have roasted seeds from a vampire melon. Vampire melons have restorative properties like a regular melon but are quick-acting and a little volatile. Mixing them with the lake water should mellow them out. Although there's a small chance that it'll make whoever ingests the seeds allergic to garlic."

I pull out some bright green pine needles from a side pocket on my backpack and begin lining the bottom of the terrarium. Carefully, I pour some of the Lake Nemi water into the small pool at its center.

"I left my mortar and pestle at home," I say, shaking

the vampire melon seeds onto a plate. "Can you crush these up?"

Sinistro gets to work on pulverizing the seeds with his tiny black paws.

"Alright, Lula," Mr. Calamoneri begins. "I'm gonna need you to open your mouth again and hum." He nods to his keyboard. "Try your best to match the note here. I'll play a series of notes that work like a spell. They'll generate the magic needed to untangle that frog." Mr. Calamoneri nods to me and holds out a shallow dish. "You can catch the frog in this. Be sure to hold it close to her chin."

Mr. Calamoneri turns back to Lula, his brown eyes warm. "It's gonna feel really weird. I'll warn you. Like your throat's all sore and scratchy. But that's normal. You'll need to keep humming through the weirdness."

"Hum through the weirdness. Sound advice," Sinistro says as he cleans his whiskers.

I roll my eyes at him and say, "Keep squashing those seeds," as I walk over to Lula and Mr. Calamoneri.

"Just try to pretend I'm not here," I say to Lula with a small smile. It's the best I can do. Even though my bedside manner's gotten better since being Mr. Calamoneri's apprentice, it's still not so great. At least I'm pretty good at faking smiles now. One time, on a house call with Rocco, I ended up getting in an argument with the patient about whether to use the Latin *vapor* or Italian *vapore* in a spell to help with allergies. Even though we're Italian, it's still *vapor* in our version of the spell because of reasons. But of course the patient's brother's friend's cousin's sister was a guaritrice in Siena and he trusted her over us. So it's better I don't say much to Lula or else I may end up scaring her.

Lula nods, her eyes large and filled with panic. She looks at Mr. Calamoneri, who pats her on the shoulder. "You can do this," he says. "I promise. It'll all be okay."

With that, Mr. Calamoneri cracks his knuckles and sidles up to his keyboard. He begins with a low chord. Lula's humming comes out in a rasp. Like leaves scraping against bricks. Mrs. and Mr. Garcia crouch down next to her, straining to hear the barely there noise. Mr. Calamoneri's fingers move to a higher note and Lula takes a deep breath before hitting it with something that sounds like a punctured balloon.

"Good job. You're doing great."

Ribbet, ribbet.

I jump at the noise. A large mass slides up Lula's neck from between her clavicles. Her skin stretches to reveal the hand of a frog. My stomach lurches. It's a gross sight, but not the first time I've seen something this bizarre. I try to keep the revulsion off my face so as not to upset Lula and steady the dish under her mouth, planting my feet firmer on the floor. I can't let her—or the frog—down.

Mr. Calamoneri picks up the pace, playing a series of quick notes. Lula matches him with her humming, the sound growing more strangled as the frog pushes and pulls inside her throat. Her face is scrunched up in deep concentration, as if the humming might possibly hurt. Every now and then a *ribbet* echoes out from her mouth and I tighten my grip on the dish.

Mrs. and Mr. Garcia have taken a few steps back from us to give some space and Sinistro sits on the edge of the kitchen table, head tilted and eyes tracking the frog's movements with interest.

"Sinistro, you can't eat this frog," I say through gritted teeth. "I'm trying to rescue it."

"Are you kidding?" He scoffs. "It's been in this poor girl's throat for who knows how long. I prefer my food free-range." He raises his chin, fur bristling with indignation. "I'm merely curious."

"Just a little longer, Lula." Mr. Calamoneri plays another flourish of notes. The song is melodic, but strange. It seems organic, as if the song is part of nature. As if it's been around longer than pianos have even been around. The song vibrates against my bones, tugging at my magic. I can feel its strength as it whirls through the air and circles around Lula. It calls to me in a way that makes my own magic feel stronger.

Mr. Calamoneri hits an especially high note and, at first, Lula struggles to meet the pitch. Then her humming breaks through, matching it with a strangled, squeaky sound. But her mouth opens wide, almost like she can no longer keep it shut and now instead of humming she's vocalizing off-key.

Ribbet. Ribbet. Ribbet.

I rear back, the dish shaking in my hand. Taking a deep breath, I regain my footing and peer into Lula's mouth. Two beady eyes twinkle from behind her tongue and molars. "Frog!" I shout. "I can see it!"

"Now, he's gonna be in bad shape, Gi," Mr. Calamoneri says as he rattles off another complex set of notes for Lula to match. "As soon as he's free—which'll likely be with the next chords—take him over to your station and do whatever you can to fix him up."

I nod, squaring my shoulders.

Mr. Calamoneri stretches his fingers over the keys and looks back at us. He asks, "Are you ready, Lula? You're doing an amazing job, but this next bit is going to be tough. Breathe through your nose and reach for the notes. These will be higher."

Lula rocks forward on her chair just a bit, her knuckles

white as she clenches the seat. But she nods. She's probably more ready than anyone for the frog to be out of her throat.

Mr. Calamoneri plays a string of notes that are higher than anything he's played yet. My gaze travels from him to Lula as she does her best to climb the octave he jumped and hum at the right pitch.

Ribbet. Ribbet. Riiiiiibbet.

Lula opens her mouth wider and the frog wriggles out past her teeth. It bangs its head on the roof of her mouth on the way out and Lula nearly bites down on its leg in her surprise. My heart aches and it takes all my willpower not to reach in and pull it out.

In a matter of seconds, though, it's struggling out from between her lips. The frog collapses on the dish, its heart beating rapidly. Lula's hum turns into a scream and her parents rush back to her side. Mr. Calamoneri also swoops in, gently nudging me out of the way. He coaxes her to drink a few sips of Gola Cura, and begins applying a thick coat of Croak Clear to her neck.

I hurry the frog over to my station and carefully begin my examination, shining a penlight in its sightless eyes and over its body. The frog is small and the skin on its neck is loose—meaning the frog must be male. The frog's green skin is mottled with blue and purple bruises and his left leg is bent in an unnatural direction. He's taking deep, gasping breaths as if struggling to get enough oxygen.

"It's alright, froggy," I whisper, while touching the tip of my finger to his head. I feel my magic brush against the frog's slippery skin, but it's not right. It depends on the creature, but usually there's a swirl of colors or a flood of emotions or images. Sometimes, it's even possible to read a creature's thoughts clearly. But I can't get through to the little frog. Like he's having trouble opening communication between us. "I'm here to help you."

Sinistro leans over the frog, eyes narrow as he takes in the poor creature. "Mr. Calamoneri wasn't kidding. It's not looking good."

"We're gonna have to go straight to the vampire melon seeds. We need to stabilize him before healing any of the topical wounds."

"They're crushed and ready to go." Sinistro nudges over a cutting board with the freshly pulverized seeds.

"Thanks!" I snatch up the jar of Lake Nemi water, pour a splash into a dish, and brush the seeds in after. I stir the mixture with a silver whisk until it starts to foam and turn into a thick, opal-hued slurry. Then, I rummage through my backpack for my medical kit and pull out a small medicine syringe. I fill it up to .5 ml and nudge the syringe between the frog's lips before pushing the potion into his mouth. With two fingers, I sit the frog up so the medicine travels down his throat and into his belly.

"Maestra Vita always says guaritori don't cure, they strengthen," I tell the frog. "And that's just what you need right now." The simple but quick-acting restorative potion made from the seeds and water should provide a boost to the frog's immunity. After a moment, his breathing begins to stabilize, but his eyes are still unfocused. I grab a dropper from my kit and fill it with more of the water, squirting just a couple drops into each eye to wash the gunk from them. The frog blinks several times as the moisture works its way around his eyes. I dab at his tears and the nasty gray goop that runs down his cheeks with a cotton swab. The frog's still not as with-it as I'd like, but the restorative potion is still working through his system.

I move on to his twisted leg. After examining it more closely, I sigh in relief at seeing it isn't broken. Just sprained. Good thing since I need to brew another batch of ossa rotte. I grab a bit of spider silk threaded with mermaid scales from my backpack. Both are excellent for healing, but the mermaid scales are particularly useful. They reinforce the spider silk's strength and are especially good at mending. Particularly anything to do with the vocal cords. Both the Gola Cura and Croak Clear Mr. Calamoneri used on Lula incorporate mermaid scales.

I cut off a frog-leg-sized piece with a pair of gold shears and smear some immortal jellyfish goo on one side. "This is what we're gonna do, froggy. We're gonna bend your leg the right way and then create a little cast. We're lucky it's just a sprain."

The frog blinks at me, and I feel him push back against my magic, trying to open up to me. But the connection isn't strong enough. He's still fighting to stay alert. I nervously chew my bottom lip before adding, "This might hurt just a bit. But it's gonna be okay. I promise." The frog turns away from me, as if he *did* understand that. "It'll be okay." I repeat as his little leg twitches.

The frog flexes his little webbed toes and his face scrunches up in pain. I roll my shoulders back. All I need to do is focus. I've taken care of creatures in worse condition than this. I slide my finger under the frog's twisted leg and tug it gently back into the correct position so the sprain heals straight.

Ribbet. Ribbet.

The frog winces again and it takes all my willpower not to just stop and leave his leg as is. But I continue to adjust his leg and then wind the silk around, making sure the jellyfish goo is pressed firmly against his skin. Magic rushes through my fingertips as I pat the cast into place, and I feel it zap like electricity into the frog's tiny leg. Not all my magic, so I won't feel exhausted, but just enough to jump-start the healing process and reinforce the other work I've done.

I flip the frog onto his belly and scoop up some more of the jellyfish goo, massaging it into his bruises. His skin begins to deepen to a greener, healthier color and the bruises go from nasty purple to a healing yellow.

"Good job, froggy. You did so well." This time, the frog's eyes sharpen on me and I feel him push back against my magic. His thoughts run together in colors and shadows. From black to red to orange and finally green. He nudges against my palm—the frog's quiet thanks for the help— and I pat his slimy head.

Carefully, I pick up the frog and put him in the terrarium. He limps over for a feast of dried grasshoppers I bought at the pet shop. He munches away, tired but in the clear.

The sound of applause draws me away from admiring the frog and I look up to see Mr. Calamoneri, Lula, and her parents staring at us.

Mr. Calamoneri's clapping his hands, grinning. "Well done, Gi! You handled that marvelously."

A flush creeps up my cheeks and I can't keep the smile from my face. "Thanks! There was a moment where I was a little worried, but froggy here was a brave patient."

"You saved him," Lula whispers. Her voice is scratchy

but at least now she can talk. "It was so cool watching you work."

"I'm glad you're feeling better."

Lula touches her throat. "Me, too. It was scary."

Mr. Calamoneri hands Mrs. and Mr. Garcia a handwritten set of instructions, along with seven vials of potion and a jar of balm. He pats Lula on the shoulder, and we all say our goodbyes. Mr. Calamoneri promises to check in with the family in a few days as I carry the terrarium out the front door, Sinistro at my heels.

"Whew, that was awesome. Really awesome," Mr. Calamoneri says as he opens the car door for me. I wrap my arms around the terrarium and watch as the frog sleeps soundly in a nest of moss and leaves. In about a week, we'll be ready to release him back into the wild. But right now, he needs rest.

Sinistro jumps into the back seat and curls up in the middle. Mr. Calamoneri slides into the driver's seat and sets off out of Garfield toward Clifton (that's where the Calamoneris live) as the oldies station plays "Superstition" by Stevie Wonder—another artist the Calamoneris love to play at home. We ride in silence for a few minutes until we get to a stoplight and Mr. Calamoneri looks at me, smiling.

"A successful day. I just wish Moss could join us more."

His eyes tighten and he adds, "I know his mood's not the greatest right now."

I stare forward, focused on the red light. "It's okay. He's not feeling well."

"If the diagnosis helps us to find the right treatment plan like we're hoping it does, maybe he'll be able to return to his apprenticeship." Mr. Calamoneri runs a hand through his hair and sighs. "I know he's suffering and, on top of that, feeling held back from his studies right now. That'll mess with your magic, and that'd be true of any witch."

I wonder if my papa had conversations like this with Rocco, about me. I didn't have an illness, but my family knew that I was unhappy, and they also didn't know how to deal with it. Neither did I, for that matter, and I think I can relate to Moss in that way. It's hard to control your magic when *your life* feels out of control, no matter what the reasons are.

"That's true," I say. "And maybe that means Moss's apprenticeship will just need to look a little different than the usual. Mrs. Calamoneri's right. Crohn's is part of Moss's life—part of all of our lives—now. Maybe some things will just have to change a bit."

I chew on my lip as I wonder how I can help Moss. I started my apprenticeship with Mr. Calamoneri just before Moss got his official diagnosis. At first, Moss and his parents were relieved and hopeful. But, after a month, as Moss's flare-ups continued—pain that took his breath away—everyone's spirits started to shift. Moss grew impatient as his stomach cramps and nausea persisted—even with the diet his doctor recommended and the medication he was given. Plus, every few days was different. Sometimes Moss would feel fine over the weekend, but the next day he'd be in so much agony he wouldn't be able to get out of bed or leave the bathroom. He'd go without eating because if he did it'd make him feel worse. His magic started to flicker, growing inconsistent. Sometimes, he was able to perform spells. But other times, there was nothing he could do to get his magic to work.

These last few weeks, it's kind of like he doesn't have the urge to try anymore, and I can't blame him. Being here, living with Moss, while he and his parents struggle, is hard. I feel like an intruder at times, and it can get awkward when everyone's upset. But I love Moss and his family. They're all doing their best to find the right path forward and sometimes that can become a bit of a maze.

The light turns green, and we zoom down the street, merging onto the highway. I look out the window, watching the trees blur together, and think of Moss, and what it means to have a calling.

3

Moss is downstairs with Fe when we get back, Prince playing on the speaker. He's sitting on the couch, his back to the garage door, so he doesn't see or hear us when we come in. On the coffee table is a large book, his veterinarian's log, a small silver cauldron, a collection of amethyst and carnelian crystals, and various glass jars filled with swirling liquids and salves. Fe paces from one edge of the coffee table to the other, her claws clicking on the wood. Whisps of a purple-and-orange smoke quickly turn a gloomy gray as they curl out of the cauldron. Moss whistles at Fe in conversation. Because she's his familiar, all I can hear is her tweet in response. He leans over his vet's log to jot something down before rubbing his stomach. Moss fiddles with his pen, tapping it on the edge of the coffee table in agitation. That's something I've noticed these past couple months about him. Whenever he's frustrated or not feeling great, it shows in his fidgeting. Moss yawns and grumbles, "I feel like garbage."

"What're you working on there, bud?" Mr. Calamoneri asks, the excitement in his voice unmistakable.

Moss jumps in his seat and whips around to stare at us. "How long have you been standing there?" He slams the book and his vet's log shut and begins stashing his supplies in his backpack.

This is the first time in a few weeks that I've seen Moss do more complex magic. Or at least attempt to. From his annoyance, it doesn't look like he's been very successful. My heart squeezes and I fight the urge to hurry over and help him. Rocco used to do that, and I found it highly annoying. But I can't help but feel hope that maybe Moss is feeling the tiniest bit better.

"We weren't spying on you or anything." I walk over to the kitchen island and put down the terrarium. The frog's just woken up and is eating some more grasshoppers. He'll need more jellyfish goo on his bruises before bedtime, but he's doing much better than he was even just an hour ago.

"I didn't accuse you of spying." Moss rolls his eyes, but he sure sounds accusatory. "You guys just caught me off guard."

Mr. Calamoneri puts both his hands up and smiles at his son. "I won't ask any questions. But I'm proud of you, Moss."

"Ugh." Moss shakes his head as he turns off the speaker. "You're both so embarrassing."

Sinistro leaps onto a stool and cleans at his whiskers. "Welcome to my life," he says even though Moss can't understand him.

Moss continues, "It'd be better if my magic just worked like it used to. And I wish I didn't feel like I had to miss going on house calls with you just because I'm worried about being close to a bathroom, or because I know I'll need more breaks than you and Giada might."

"I'm sorry you're so frustrated, but your Crohn's isn't going to go away. There'll always be days, maybe even weeks, when you have flare-ups," Mr. Calamoneri says as he puts his bag on the kitchen table.

"I know it won't go away. I'm okay with that part." Moss tilts his head back and sighs. After a moment, he looks at his dad again and says, "My stomach hurts. It's bad today and I feel shaky because of it. It feels like I've had to push pause on my life."

Fe lands on Moss's shoulder and he runs a finger over her feathers. I think about Moss missing out on the house calls, and what Mrs. Calamoneri said this morning. What if the best way to support Moss is something none of us has even thought of yet?

"We'll get there," Mr. Calamoneri says, walking closer toward Moss and placing a hand on his shoulder. "It'll work out."

Moss doesn't say anything and goes over to the fridge for a glass of water before walking back into the living room and sitting down on the couch.

My phone vibrates from my backpack and a picture of Alessia standing in front of the Mediterranean Sea pops up on the screen. I immediately remember her text from this morning and pick up. "Alessia! Ciao!"

"Ciao!" Alessia's voice erupts from the phone, and I can't help but grin. "It's been a billion years since we talked. How are you?"

"It's only been like a week since our last phone call. But I'm good! Just got back from this really cool house call."

"You'll have to tell me about it in person because guess what!" Alessia is practically shouting now. "The Pulaskis and I are coming to New Jersey tonight!"

"Ahh!" I scream, causing both Moss and Mr. Calamoneri to look at me in alarm. "What? Why?"

"We were called about a lone unicorn roaming around the tarmac at Teterboro Airport. Usually unicorns travel in groups, called a blessing. But this one's lost its family and we're going to care for it at the sanctuary," Alessia explains.

The Pulaskis are teaching her how to build bonds with unicorns and how to utilize their magic without harm. Now Alessia's even hoping to open her own unicorn sanctuary back in Italy, which would be the first of its kind there. Unicorns are incredibly rare creatures, their magic used by all streghe. But they're nearly extinct and constantly in danger of poachers.

"Do you and the Calamoneris want to meet up with us?" Alessia asks. "You'd all get to see the unicorn."

I gasp, excitement thrums through me, and I yell, "Yes!" A thought occurs to me, and I can hear my mamma telling me to mind my manners. I pause. "Oh, but wait. I gotta ask first. Hang on." I pull away from my phone and call, "Mr. Calamoneri! My best friend, Alessia, is gonna be in Teterboro tonight to pick up a unicorn with her host family. She said we could see the unicorn. Can we go?" I'm bouncing on the balls of my feet, too energized to stand still. "Please?"

"A unicorn, eh?" Mr. Calamoneri laughs. "Of course we can go. It's not every day you get to see a unicorn."

"THANK YOU!" I yell to Mr. Calamoneri, pumping my fist

in the air. "Alessia!" I say back into the phone. "We get to see you and the unicorn!"

"Amazing! I can't wait to see you!" Alessia says she'll text their flight details and, after making plans with Mr. Calamoneri, we agree to go out to dinner at a diner nearby before seeing the unicorn.

I hang up with Alessia and squeal. I twirl from the kitchen into the living room where Moss is still sitting, Fe now perched on his shoulder. "A unicorn! Moss, we're gonna see a real live unicorn!"

He shrugs. "It's cool, I guess."

"You *guess*." I squint at him. "Madonna mia! This is huge."

"How do you know?" Moss challenges. "Have you ever seen a unicorn before?"

"Well, no…"

"Then you don't know for sure."

"You're so annoying." I roll my eyes, face heating up. "It's a unicorn. Of *course* it's gonna be incredible."

He shakes his head. "*I'm* annoying? I'm not the one yelling my head off about unicorns."

"Oh, come *onnnn*!"

"Fine." Moss's lips quirk up. He tosses a pillow at me. "Maybe it's a little better than cool."

"Exactly." I snatch the pillow off the ground and throw it back at him. "You'll be so impressed."

"Yeah, yeah. We'll see," Moss laughs. But I can see the ghost of a smile on his face. Maybe this is just what he needs. The inspiration that'll give him a boost.

We arrive at Big Ang's Diner a couple miles from Teterboro Airport. The small, aluminum-sided building is nestled between two busy streets. As the sun sets over the highway in bursts of red, purple, and pink, the diner's orange-and-blue-neon sign hums to life. Even though I miss Positano, we don't have anything like a New Jersey diner. There's nothing better than the huge menu with hundreds of options; the vinyl booths that squeak when you slide into them; the case of delicious cakes and pastries up at the front. And, my favorite, the disco fries. They're fresh salty fries piled high with savory brown gravy and melty, ooey-gooey mozzarella. Disco fries are the best food I've ever eaten, and I'll miss them so much when I go back to Italy.

I adjust the strap of Sinistro's carrier on my shoulder. Fe's hiding in Moss's backpack. Technically animals aren't allowed in any diners (or really any restaurants), but they're good at staying quiet and will be given food for their troubles.

We settle into a big booth near the back of the diner and the waitress brings us cups of water with lemon and a stack of thick spiral-ringed menus. I lean against the back of the booth, inhaling the cinnamon and honey of the fresh baklava baking in the kitchen. Heaven is a New Jersey diner, and I can't wait for Alessia to experience it. Moss fiddles with his rolled silverware. I nudge his shoulder, grinning. "You're gonna love Alessia. She's the best."

Moss shrugs and places his paper napkin on his lap. "I'm sure she'll be fine."

I glare at him, but he only smirks, which annoys me even more.

"Looks like she might be here," Mrs. Calamoneri says, peeking around the booth and at the entrance.

I turn around in time to see Alessia and the Pulaskis walking toward us. Mrs. Pulaski's hair is bright red and curly, and her eyes are a light green. Her skin's white and speckled with lots of freckles. She wears jeans and a simple, long-sleeved blue shirt under a black puffer jacket, staring at us from behind a pair of gold-rimmed glasses. Mr. Pulaski's blond hair reflects the fluorescent diner lights, and his eyes are a dark brown. He has a scruffy red-blond beard covering most of his white face. He's dressed similarly to his wife in a pair of well-worn jeans, a button-down flannel, and a navy jacket. Alessia is the odd one out in her pink jean jacket, blue dress, gray tights, and fuzzy lilac boots. Her brown hair is still cut in the same curly bob, but her olive skin's pale like mine after living in a super cold and dark city for months. A huge smile spreads across her face as she catches sight of us.

"Giada!" She runs toward the booth, and I pop out of it in time for us to meet in a hug.

"Alessia," I say. "I missed you!"

"I missed you, too." She pulls back, turning to the Pulaskis before addressing Moss and his parents. "Ciao, I'm Alessia. These are my host parents, but I think you know them already?"

"It's good to see you both again," Mrs. Calamoneri says. "It's been a while."

"Too long," Mr. Pulaski agrees.

"I'm Giada," I say, shaking Mr. and Mrs. Pulaski's hands.

"We've heard so much about you and your adventures with Alessia," Mrs. Pulaski laughs.

I introduce Alessia and the Pulaskis to Moss. He nods to them, smiling, but doesn't say much.

"Is that Sinistro?" Alessia asks as we all slide into the booth, eyeing the leopard print carrier next to me.

"It sure is. He wants to see the unicorn, too."

Sinistro meows and paws against the zipper. I open it just a little so he can stick his head out. He blinks up at Alessia, head tilted to the side, and she wiggles her fingers at him.

"Moss is like me," I explain.

"You're a magical veterinarian?" Alessia's eyes widen. "Do you have a familiar, too?"

"A dove named Ofelia." Moss smiles and nods to the little white bird nested quietly on top of his backpack. "Fe for short."

"Oh, hello there," Alessia whispers to Fe, who chirps back in response.

"She's kind of shy sometimes," Moss explains.

"That's okay. I am, too," Alessia says. Moss's smile widens and I can't help but smile with him. Alessia's the best at making people feel comfortable. I knew Moss would like her.

The waitress stops by to take our orders and after she leaves, Mrs. Calamoneri asks in a low voice, "Can you tell us anything about the unicorn you're looking for?"

The Pulaskis look at each other before Mrs. Pulaski begins, "Well, we've heard it looks like a female unicorn. Female unicorns tend to be smaller and have white hair and manes. Male unicorns have silver hair and manes and are much larger."

"It's because male unicorns are a lot like male peacocks or lions," Alessia explains. "They flip their silver manes around when in the presence of female unicorns to attract them."

"And we've also heard that she appears younger," Mrs. Pulaski adds. "Maybe just a few years old."

46

"How do you know?" I ask, taking a sip of my water.

"Well, it's tricky. Every century, a unicorn sheds its horn and grows a new one. An older unicorn *can* be mistaken for a young one if they're in the midst of regrowing their horn, because it takes two to three years for it to fully form. However, only a young unicorn—one born in the past five years—will have a pink horn. We've been told this unicorn's horn appears pink."

"Fascinating," I breathe. My fingers itch for my veterinarian's log and it takes all my effort not to pull it from my backpack and start scribbling notes.

There aren't many books on unicorns as they're so uncommon. The books that do exist are from the Middle Ages and are positively grotesque in the way they speak about capturing and killing unicorns for their hearts, blood, and other parts. The Pulaskis are doing what they can to educate other streghe on the nature of unicorns because they think if there is more information out there on how to successfully gather their horns or hair without harming them, fewer people will be inclined to poach.

"Unicorns can live up to one thousand years," Mr. Pulaski says. "So that means a unicorn may shed its horn up to ten times. It grows a paler pink each time until it's an opal color."

The waitress returns with our food, and we settle into

silence as we all eat. Alessia begins cutting her stack of chocolate chip pancakes into neat squares before covering them in warm maple syrup. Moss stabs at a piece of grilled chicken, making sure to scoop up a bit of ziti and zucchini on the fork, too. I give Sinistro a French fry covered in gravy, which he munches on happily, before I say, "So do you have any old unicorns at your sanctuary?"

"We have two," Mr. Pulaski says before taking a bite of his spanakopita and swallowing. "A male and female pair. They bonded centuries ago and haven't been apart since." He takes another bite of food and continues, "They've actually had two offspring while in our care."

"How do you know their ages?" Moss asks.

"You count the spirals on their horns. Kind of like the rings inside a tree," Mrs. Pulaski explains with a warm smile. "Each spiral counts toward a single year."

After that, the subject changes to the last time the Pulaskis and Calamoneris saw each other, at a fixer conference in Taos a couple years ago. They reminisce over the warm weather and fun dinners out with other fixers. After a while, the waitress returns with the check, and we all get up to leave, Mr. Calamoneri paying for our meal at the register on the way out.

"Are you excited yet, Moss?" I ask as we settle into our car. Mrs. Calamoneri follows behind the Pulaskis' rental truck, rigged with a horse trailer, for their long drive back to Chicago.

"I'm getting there," he says while letting Fe out of his backpack and petting her head. "I'll admit, few things are cooler than a unicorn."

Happiness swells in my chest and I can't keep the smile from my face. I see Mrs. and Mr. Calamoneri exchange a look, both smiling as well.

It doesn't take us long to reach Teterboro Airport. We turn in near a squat white building with a wall of windows facing the tarmac. A man with a shiny, bald white head wearing a white button-down shirt and gray slacks greets us at the door with a smile.

"You're the Pulaskis?" he asks.

"Yes." Mr. Pulaski gives the man a handshake. "We brought our friends with us," he adds, gesturing to the Calamoneris and me. "You must be Vince."

"The one and only!"

At the diner, the Pulaskis told us we'd be meeting with a man named Vince, a line service technician who works at Teterboro. They explained that a line service technician makes sure airplanes are safe. While not a strega himself, he knows about witches and magic because his aunt and cousins are witches. It always makes things easier when people with jobs like Vince's know about the magical world. Papa and Rocco prefer working with doctors who know about guaritori since it means there'll be fewer questions.

"Nice to meet you," Mr. Pulaski says. "We're very eager to meet the unicorn."

"Excellent." Vince opens the door to the building and leads us straight through another door out to the tarmac where he nods to a white SUV. "We'll have to drive out to the old control tower. That's where she's been hiding. You can drive up to the fence by the tower—it's about a mile down the road. You can't miss it."

Mr. Pulaski hops back into his truck while the rest of us squeeze into the SUV. Vince drives us down the tarmac at a breakneck speed.

"We appreciate you arranging for us to leave directly from Teterboro," Mrs. Pulaski says. "Hopefully we won't take too long coaxing her to come with us."

Vince comes to an abrupt stop, causing Sinistro to fall off my lap and onto the floor.

"Why is it always me getting jostled around?" Sinistro complains as I open the car door to let him out.

The night air is heavy with the scent of rain and, in the distance, thunder rumbles. A storm's on the way. We walk up to a tall building that kind of reminds me of the Torre di Apollo back in Positano—except much more utilitarian.

The old control tower is a faded white with streaks of rust around the base. The only windows are all the way at the top where they cover each wall from head to toe. Weeds grow around the path leading up to a padlocked door.

Mr. Pulaski pulls up with his lights off and Vince unlocks a gate to let him through. He parks and joins us by the control tower's door.

Vince pulls out a flashlight, but Mrs. Pulaski stops him, saying, "Unicorns don't like artificial light. Here." She presses her palms together and her skin glows a warm yellow. In her hands are two balls of light. It's a simple bit of magic that doesn't require a lot of energy, but there's no denying how cool it looks. Vince's eyebrows rise and he gives a low whistle.

"Magic always throws me for a loop," he murmurs, wiping at his brow.

"It's convenient, though," Mrs. Pulaski laughs. "Now, let's find our unicorn."

We circle the control tower as a group. "She's been hanging out in the bushes. I think she knows the control tower's empty. It's usually quiet over here."

Vince leads us over to the bushes and the Pulaskis walk toward them with cautious steps. I hold my breath, standing on my tiptoes to see if I can spy any hint of the unicorn. Moss and Alessia wait next to me, and I can feel the excitement threading through the air between us. Sinistro curls between my legs impatiently and Fe hops from Moss's left shoulder to his right.

But when Mr. Pulaski turns around, he's frowning. "She isn't here."

"Could she be hiding somewhere else?" Mr. Calamoneri asks.

Vince scratches the back of his neck. "This is the only place I've seen her. And there haven't been any reports about other spottings at the airport."

"Unicorns tend to stay in one place if they deem it safe," Mrs. Pulaski explains. She lets one of the orange flames in her palm snuff out before adjusting her glasses. "I imagine the constant noise from the planes would also keep her from moving too much."

A bad feeling creeps up from my belly. Something's not right here. I inhale and press my own palms together to create balls of light. "Let's spread out and search the area."

Moss, Alessia, and Mrs. Calamoneri all create their own light sources, and we fan out in separate directions around the control tower.

"Could she have gotten inside?" I hear Alessia ask as I walk counterclockwise from the bushes.

"No, the door's always locked," Vince explains.

"What are you thinking, Giada?" Sinistro asks as he trots next to me.

I press my lips in a firm line, the bad feeling now gnawing at my bones. But before I can respond, Moss's voice cuts through the air.

"I found something!"

Alessia, Sinistro, and I hurry to where Moss is standing on the other side of the bushes. Glimmering in Moss's light are long strands of white hair hanging from a branch. And right below shine six pennies—each one tail side up.

A calling card I might not have paid any mind a few months ago. But one that now sends a shiver down my spine.

"What does it mean?" Moss asks.

Six pennies. Tail side up. Mocking me, almost, with their brightness. A clear warning of bad luck.

Memories I thought I'd buried deep down come twisting up out of the darkness. Flashes of my kitchen dripping in olive oil. Bursts of Rocco locked away in a golden cage, his eyes flat and shoulders slumped. The Madre del Malocchio threatening to eat my brother's heart and steal his magic.

"Giada?" I feel Alessia's hand on my shoulder, snapping me out of my thoughts. "What's wrong?"

"It's the same as last time," I say. "The Streghe del Malocchio are at it again."

4

Mrs. Pulaski paces from the kitchen to the living room and back again so many times I'm afraid she'll wear a hole in the floor. The blue light of dawn begins to pool in through the windows.

Moss, Alessia, and I went to bed a few hours after we got back from Teterboro and, even though the Calamoneris offered the mother-in-law suite over the garage to the Pulaskis, the adults stayed up through the night to volley the same questions and theories between each other like a beach ball near ready to burst. When we come downstairs—way too early, but unable to stay in bed any longer—they're still at it.

"Do you know of any poachers who may have had the same intel as you?" Mrs. Calamoneri asks again, hands clutching a mug of tea. "Did Vince say something to someone else?"

Mrs. Pulaski shakes her head, leaning on the kitchen island by the other adults. "I don't think he would have. He has witches in his family. He respects magic."

"And it wouldn't make sense to agree to us *and* poachers coming out to the airfield at the same time," Mr. Pulaski adds.

Moss, Alessia, and I sit on the couch. Alessia continues to run her fingers through the strands of unicorn hair, tears in her eyes. Sinistro lies in her lap, occasionally rubbing his head into her arm for comfort. I hold tight to the six pennies in my fist—so tight they turn warm and I can smell copper.

Fe chirrups something next to Moss's ear and he whistles back a low tune. I bump him with my shoulder and open my palm to show him the pennies again. "I'm telling you, these are a warning," I whisper, eyeing the adults as they talk in the kitchen. They can't know about my theory. It's too dangerous for them. "The Streghe del Malocchio stole the unicorn and are trying to contact me. Again. This is not the work of a poacher."

"How can you be so sure, though?" Moss asks. "Pennies end up on the ground all the time."

"*Six* extremely shiny pennies? All tail side up? Next to an abandoned control tower?" My voice raises higher with each question and finally I lean back into the couch in a huff. "Not likely."

"But a coven of fairy-tale witches trying to communicate with you is?" Moss crosses his arms over his chest and shakes his head.

"They have before. I told you all about Rocco and everything." I nod to Alessia, who's now petting Sinistro's fluffy head. "Alessia was there, too. She saw them."

"The Streghe del Malocchio are real, Moss," she says, her voice watery. "They even tried stealing a gryphon when we were down there. Them taking the unicorn is believable."

Moss frowns. "Okay. I don't think you're making up a story." He eyes the adults as they continue to discuss the possibility of poachers before saying, "It's just—what are the odds that this would happen again? Besides, it'd have to be a different coven of Streghe del Malocchio, too, since the ones you dealt with were under Positano. That's far away from New Jersey. Do you really think a separate coven would steal a unicorn and leave a calling card of pennies like some weird cartoon villain?"

I shrug. "I didn't say they were original."

"They probably heard about what happened in Malafi," Alessia adds.

"And were bold enough to try it again?" Moss presses.

"Listen. I'm not here to debate why they'd do it," I begin, carefully laying the six pennies on the coffee table in a circle. I rub my palms on my pajama pants and continue, "I just think everything points to them. Now. The question is if you two are gonna come with me."

"Hold on. Come with you *where*?" Moss asks.

"To find the Streghe del Malocchio, of course." I hop off the couch, snatch my backpack off the ground, and start heading toward the stairs. Moss's parents and the Pulaskis are still huddled over the kitchen island talking about the unicorn. "You don't have to come with us, but Sinistro and I are going."

Alessia looks at Moss and then back to me. "Let's take our time, Giada. We should slow down, eat something, use the bathroom, and make sure we're all feeling okay and have everything we need before we go charging off. *If* we go charging off."

My cheeks grow hot. I know I have a tendency to blow through things when I get excited about saving magical animals. But Moss might need to take a beat before running out of the house with me with no notice. Alessia's so much better with people than I am—I'm grateful she said something. "Okay, sorry, let's eat something and discuss."

Alessia quickly navigates between the adults and grabs some bananas from the kitchen island, joining Moss and me back in the living room.

Moss unpeels his banana and asks, "Shouldn't we at least try to tell my parents and the Pulaskis what's happening?"

"Adults never listen." I roll my eyes, remembering how Zia Clementina didn't believe me when Rocco went missing. "They *never* think it's the Streghe del Malocchio."

"But my parents heard your story. I'm sure the Pulaskis have, too."

I think of my own parents and zia locked up in golden cages next to Alessia's and Rocco's. The image is burned into my memories and plays frequently in my nightmares. My parents and zia weren't even involved—the Streghe del Malocchio sought them out. I don't want to risk the Calamoneris or Pulaskis getting roped into this and ending up the same way. I've put enough people in danger to last a lifetime.

"The less they know, the better," I say. "We want to keep them as far away from the Streghe del Malocchio as possible."

Sunlight filters between the blinds as dawn turns to

day. "We gotta get ready," I say, before locking eyes with Moss. "What should we pack? If you're coming, that is. You don't have to. Seriously. No pressure."

"I'll bring my snacks and water, and some magical vet supplies, too. I really want to come, but before I agree to this, you should know I'll need to take breaks to rest, and I'll need to use the bathroom sometimes. More often than you both will," Moss explains. "So we might not be able to go as fast as you want. Can you accept that?"

"Yes," I say, and I mean it. I want them with me on this journey. *Both* of them.

Moss looks back at his parents and the Pulaskis before turning toward me again and asks, "Where exactly are we going?"

A grin spreads across my lips. "We're going to Olde Yorque."

Moss and Alessia look at each other before looking back at me, confusion on their faces.

"When I first got to Malafi—the city underneath Positano—there was a sign pointing in all different directions, to all the other cities-beneath-cities. They exist all over the world," I explain. "Olde Yorque is the city under New York."

"Olde Yorque?" Alessia scrunches her nose. "That's a silly name."

"How do you expect us to get there?" Moss asks. "Do

you even know where the entrance to the underground city is?"

I gesture for Moss to keep his voice down, eyeing the adults. They appear to be jotting down a list of some sort, not paying us any attention. But still, I nod for us to go upstairs to my bedroom. Once there, I close the door and immediately begin rummaging through my closet.

"We'll take the train, of course. Like we have before," I say over my shoulder while searching through various jars of tonics, potions, and raw ingredients. What could we need against the Streghe del Malocchio this time? What kind of bargain will they request? Worry churns in my stomach, flipping and flopping. Guaritori never make bargains with Streghe del Malocchio. Even though I'm not a guaritrice anymore, I still hate the idea of doing it. But— and I know this from experience—it's impossible to get anything from them without one.

"Take the train?" Moss repeats. "We can't take the train alone. We're only thirteen. A conductor will stop us and ask too many questions."

"Then we'll take the bus." I shrug, tossing a jar of pixie wings into my backpack.

"No can do, Giada. The bus is worse. My mom and dad don't want me going to Port Authority by myself."

"You'd be with me and Alessia."

"You know that doesn't count."

I pull out the set of seven gryphon feathers that Mamma Gryphon let me take from her a few months ago and an idea pops in my head. "Where are the nearest cliffs?"

"Um…" Moss scratches his head. "Weehawken, I think? But that's like half an hour away. Why?"

Alessia notices the feathers in my hand and shakes her head. "Oh, no. Giada, you aren't thinking what I think you're thinking."

"I'm thinking *exactly* that."

Sinistro stops cleaning his fur to stare at me. "I'm not riding on another gryphon."

The Calamoneris and Pulaskis finally stopped talking to take naps, and we took a quick nap of our own to catch up on sleep before heading out. We even ate a proper breakfast, and the adults were still sound asleep. Moss wanted to leave a note, but I insisted that they really shouldn't know where we're going—we can't risk them getting involved. And, anyway, the last time I snuck out on a secret mission, I left a note for my zia and she didn't even see it. Plus, if we're lucky, the Calamoneris and Pulaskis will sleep the whole day and we'll be back before they even realize we've left. They didn't go to bed last night, after all.

Even though we took a bus to Weehawken, Moss refused to break his mom's rule about Port Authority, so we jumped off before the Lincoln Tunnel.

Now we stand in Hamilton Park, overlooking the Hudson River. From here, New York City seems so close. Like we could simply hop across the water and be there.

Sinistro looks down from the cliffs at the cars on the road below and the inky blue river. "I can't believe I'm riding on another gryphon," he says regretfully.

"Just squeeze your eyes shut and think of the ground," I tell him.

"Careening and crashing into the ground."

I scratch between his shoulders and laugh. "That wasn't the visualization I quite had in mind."

"So what do we do now? How do you summon a gryphon?" Moss asks, kicking a rock through the fence and watching it tumble down the cliff face. "And how will we even know where to go when we get into the city?"

"Well, the gryphons should know about the Streghe del Malocchio. At least, the ones in Positano did. They can tell us where to go."

"They might be able to tell us about the unicorns, too," Moss says. "Magical creatures in New Jersey are big gossips. They know everything about everything since they all live so close together."

"That's great. We really need all the help we can get—

and here's how you summon a gryphon. Watch and learn!" I walk closer to the cliff's edge and place my hands on the fence's railing. Taking a deep breath, I whistle the tune Papa Gryphon taught me. The noise echoes from the cliffs, carries on the wind, and moves down toward the river.

A few minutes pass and there's nothing. The trees rustle. A dog barks. Cars honk their horns. But no gryphons emerge from their hiding places.

Alessia drags herself up to the railing. She swallows hard, terrified of heights, as she scans the waterfront from the apartment complex to the steak house and shopping center. "Where are they?"

"Gryphons can create invisible shields. Maybe they're flying toward us right now, but are invisible?" I say, but Alessia just arches an eyebrow. It doesn't even sound convincing to me. "Maybe I should try whistling again?"

"Are you sure there are gryphons in New Jersey?" she says.

I shrug. "Not entirely."

"I'll be honest. I've never heard of gryphons living here." Moss joins us by the railing and fiddles with his backpack's straps.

"Then why didn't you say something earlier?" Alessia asks.

"I mean, I think I know something that does live on

these cliffs," Moss explains. "Just not sure if they'll respond to that whistle."

"What lives here?" Alessia tugs at her short curls, her eyes wide. "Are they dangerous?"

Moss shrugs. "Probably not. Here, let me try something. I saw this call in a YouTube video for the creatures I *think* hang around here."

"You're trusting a video you saw online?" I ask, crossing my arms.

"Oh, come on." Moss waves his hand through the air. "Not all tech's bad. Try stepping into the twenty-first century."

He places his pinkie fingers in his mouth and then hesitates, looking at Fe, who is standing on his shoulder. She titters, tilting her head to the side. Moss drops his hands and whistles back, his eyebrows furrowed as he communicates with Fe. She presses her forehead against his temple and coos. Moss smiles sheepishly, explaining, "I'm a little nervous to do the call, but Fe's hyping me up."

Moss takes several deep, slow breaths, and closes his eyes. He puts his pinkies in his mouth once more and I can feel the faintest rumbling of his magic in the air. It's subtle and soft, like the electricity in the air before a rainstorm. And then he lets out the loudest, shriekiest whistle I've ever heard. I place my hands over my ears, the sound practically puncturing my eardrums. It's not at all like the gryphons' melodic call.

The sound echoes across the cliffs and we search for any sign of the mysterious creature Moss called upon. Then, a noise breaks through the quiet.

Neeeeiiiigh.

"What on earth was that?" I ask, leaning over the railing to get a better look at whatever's headed our way. My heart thrashes against my rib cage and blood pumps in my ears. I feel Sinistro tuck himself between my feet.

"I did it!" Moss yells from behind me. I look over my shoulder and he's pumping his fist in the air. A smile tugs at my lips at the sight.

Neeeiiigh. Snort.

My smile immediately drops and Moss goes quiet. The noise is closer this time, coming from a row of parked cars. I push off from the railing, and tiptoe toward the noise.

Snort. Snort. Snort.

I jump back, nearly bumping into Moss as one of the strangest-looking creatures I've ever seen waddles out from behind the trees.

It has the head of a horse, with a flowing black mane, shiny black fur, and two large horns sticking out from its forehead. But it's *not* a horse. Humongous leather wings jut out from its kangaroo-like body and a hooked tail whips through the air. The creature stands on a pair of hooves extending from spindly, crooked legs. And it has short arms with long claws that it keeps clacking together.

Moss, Alessia, and I blink at the odd creature for several moments before Moss doubles over laughing.

"What?" I ask, heat creeping up my cheeks. "Why are you laughing?"

"Y-you…thought…" Moss takes a deep breath to settle his fit of giggles and tries again. "You thought you were calling a gryphon!"

Alessia looks with apprehension. "What is it?"

"I *knew* there were no gryphons in New Jersey. The creatures here are different than the ones you've got." Moss sighs, wiping a tear from his eye. *"This—"* he gestures to the creature and grins "—is a Jersey Devil. Jersey's favorite cryptid."

The Jersey Devil stares at us with its beady black eyes and shakes out its mane. No creature is ugly—*ugly's* a lazy way to describe things. Nothing in this world is ugly. And the Jersey Devil is no exception. It's simply different. A little bizarre, but what isn't? I've never seen a creature quite like it. All I want to do is pull out my vet's log to draw up a sketch.

Neeeeiiiigh. Snort. Neeeeiiiigh.

"I've never seen one in person," Moss says. "But I've got

tons of New Jersey folklore books that talk about them. Most Jersey Devils live in the Pine Barrens down south."

"It's just not what I was expecting." I tap my foot on the ground, a little annoyed but willing to go with the flow if it can get us to the city. "But it's pretty cool."

Alessia crouches down to pet Sinistro's head and says, "Can you just talk to it and see if it can help us?"

The Jersey Devil sniffs the air and snorts again before slowly coming closer. Alessia scrambles several steps back, but Moss and I move forward. I look at him and grin. "Have you ever communicated with a creature?" I ask.

"Besides Fe?" I nod and he tilts his head, grabbing his water bottle from the pocket on his backpack and taking a few long sips. "Only a couple times…once in school and another time in my apprenticeship. Before everything got put on pause."

"Do you want to try now?"

Moss eyes the Jersey Devil with apprehension. "Jersey Devils are kind of creepy. You don't know the story about them, do you?"

I shrug, pulling out my own water bottle and drinking. "No and I don't really care. So many creatures have bad reps for no reason. Part of our job is to figure out what's true and what isn't."

"Can we do it together? I know I did the call, but that didn't take nearly as much magic as this would."

"Sure." I smile. "It's always easier with a partner."

We approach the Jersey Devil. Its wide eyes are fixed on us. I take Moss's hand and, carefully, bring it up to just behind the creature's wing. I place my own hand next to his and close my eyes, inhaling deeply. The magic bubbles up from my belly and I feel the familiar sensation of it swirling up my spine, all the way into my fingertips. I press my pinkie against Moss's and sense his magic waking up. It's quieter, slower than it was even just moments ago. But his magic stirs and presses against the Jersey Devil's alongside mine. Then it kicks up even more and feels different than I expected. Where my magic's sharp and nimble like a figure skater dancing across the ice, his is round, soft, and almost bouncy.

But then his magic starts to roll away, as if he's losing focus. Moss readjusts his hand and starts to breathe a little deeper. I look at him from the corner of my eye and I notice sweat forming on his brow as he scrunches his eyes tighter. Finally, I lose my sense of his magic entirely, and Moss groans, throwing his head back.

He drops his hand and looks at me, his face flushing. "I almost had it, but I think I need a break to recharge before doing anything else. I'm not able to do this much magic again so soon."

I smile. "That's okay. I can take this one and let you both know what he says."

Moss nods and stands with Alessia. He searches in his backpack, grabbing a baggie of homemade peanut butter cookies. He offers a couple to Alessia, who happily takes them before they both dig in.

I turn back to the Jersey Devil, focusing on communicating with him. I nudge against his magic, asking permission. He responds, and surprise jolts through me because it's different from what I'd expected. The Jersey Devil's way of communicating is not like the gryphons' or mermaids', who communicated through feelings, and not words. Instead, the Jersey Devil has an inner voice. While not uncommon, it's rare. Usually seen in older, more ancient creatures. It's a whisper that scratches against my brain. A low and haunting sound that reminds me of ghouls wandering through forests and a crackling fire at midnight.

Who are you? Why did you call to me? the voice rasps.

Excitement churns up with my magic and I respond aloud, "We're streghe in search of the Streghe del Malocchio. Can you help us?"

We do not associate with the Streghe del Malocchio.

"But do you know how to find them?"

Why do you seek them?

"What's he saying?" Moss asks between mouthfuls of cookie.

I repeat what the Jersey Devil told me, keeping my eyes on the creature.

"Tell him about the unicorn," Moss says, moving closer to us. "Maybe they know about unicorns around here?"

"We believe they stole a unicorn," I say. "Do you know anything about the unicorns in the area?"

The Jersey Devil's eyes shift to Moss and Alessia, and he snorts. *I can understand the other humans. You do not need to speak for them.*

"Oh! He says he can understand humans! You can talk to him directly, and I can translate for him." This isn't exactly uncommon, but you never know. Some creatures are more easily able to understand humans than others. Take familiars—because they already communicate directly with their streghe, they're better at this than most. But it's still a surprise.

The Jersey Devil's gaze lands on me once more as he answers the question. *Unicorns live in hiding just like every other magical creature in New Jersey. Rather than fight over territory, we help each other thrive and stay safe against humans.*

I translate, and then Moss cuts in, asking, "So why is everyone afraid of you all?"

The Jersey Devil swivels his head around to look at Moss and snorts before saying, *The rumors aren't true. All we want to do is eat, sleep, and mind our business.*

I relay his response and scritch the Jersey Devil just underneath his wing.

Neigh. He closes his eyes and rolls out his shoulders, lips curling.

"See? He's just a big, sweet bambino!" I tell Moss before returning to my questions about the unicorn. "Has there been anything fishy with the other unicorns in North Jersey?"

The Jersey Devil stares at me for a long time. My magic continues to mingle with the creature's, pushing and pulling against one another's. Finally, he begins to communicate again.

There's an evil lurking. Something's been destroying extraordinary animals and plants. We've noticed our numbers dwindling. The loss is staggering.

"Madonna mia." I quickly explain what he said to Moss and Alessia. Tears prick at my eyes. All the missing creatures that were torn away from their families and friends. What a horrible thing to do. "This is worse than we thought."

"Is it the Streghe del Malocchio?" Moss asks.

The Jersey Devil kicks up some dirt. *I don't know. There are rumors that it's humans. That they're using ingredients*

from the stolen creatures and plants to create medicine for
humans at a rate that isn't sustainable.

I translate and Moss moves closer, an eyebrow raised. "What kind of medicine?"

I don't know.

I shake my head, telling them his response before adding, "I bet the Streghe del Malocchio are helping them in some way. We'll find out and put a stop to it."

"I don't know, Giada." Moss nudges me and whispers, "What if something like this could help with my Crohn's?"

My heart breaks a little at the hope in Moss's eyes. I understand why he has to ask. But I press my lips together in a firm line because I already know that as a fellow healer of animals, he'll understand why we can't go down that road.

"I know," Moss says. "None of this is fair. Killing any animals and plants—let alone magical ones—for their resources could make them go extinct. And there's no way of knowing if whatever magical medicine they're making would even work. Considering the lengths they're going to in order to make it, it probably wouldn't be an affordable option for most people anyway." He takes a deep breath and looks at the Jersey Devil, his expression soft. "But it's a passing thought I can't help but have, you know? I've got medicine on the brain these days."

I nod. Alessia moves closer to us and takes Moss's hand for just a moment, squeezing it and then letting go.

I know we all get it, but he's right. We don't know if the magical medicine would even work—besides everything Moss pointed out, there's the fact that poached ingredients aren't nearly as powerful as the ones that are found left behind or taken from creatures who give them willingly. I tear my eyes away from Moss to look back at the creature and say, "We need your help if you can give it to us."

How do I know I can trust you? he huffs.

"I promise you can trust us," I plea, nodding to Moss and Alessia. "We've helped animals before."

Moss adds, "Yeah, you can trust us. We're magical vets. The dove and cat are our familiars."

"I'm a guaritrice, but I work at a unicorn sanctuary," Alessia chimes in. "I consider it my duty to protect them."

The Jersey Devil looks between us. *If you plan to stop this, we will help you.*

Light fills my chest and I beam at Alessia and Moss. "He says if we plan to stop this, the Jersey Devils will help us!"

"We do," Moss says.

"We will do everything we can!" Alessia says.

The Jersey Devil stomps his foot in a rhythmic pattern. *Tap…tap…tap. Tap. Tap.*

Out from the trees emerge more Jersey Devils. Some have goat's heads instead of horse's. Some are short and rotund while others are tall and lanky. Some are white, others gray, and still others brown and black. My magic tingles in their presence. All of them are completely mesmerizing.

What is it you need? the Jersey Devil communicates.

"A ride into the city. To where the Streghe del Malocchio's world connects to ours."

The Jersey Devil turns back to the others and neighs at them. A white one with gray spots responds with a shake of its head and a huff. The Jersey Devil turns back to us, his magic radiating against ours. *We don't know where that is but will bring you to someone who might.*

5

It's cold all the way up above the Hudson River. The wind whips at our cheeks turning them raw and red. Sinistro stays snug between my legs, his claws piercing my jeans.

"Why are we always so far off the ground?" he grumbles. "I'm starting to think you like traveling by winged beast."

I throw my head back, laughing, and scritch the fur between his shoulders.

"It'll be okay," I yell over the howling wind. I readjust my grip on the Jersey Devil's long mane and wipe a tear from my eye. "We'll be there in no time. Wherever *there* is."

"Won't someone notice us?" Alessia hollers from a gray-and-white-speckled Jersey Devil a few feet to the left of mine. She has her eyes squeezed shut and her arms flung around the creature's long neck. Alessia's never been good with heights. She told me she spent her entire plane ride to Chicago with her head under a blanket and her cornicello gripped tight in her fist.

Moss shakes his head. He's riding on a brown Jersey Devil, Fe nested between the creature's goatlike horns. "According to the legends, Jersey Devils are always confused for birds. Plus, it seems like they've adapted to their surroundings like a lot of other magical creatures."

"What's that mean?" Alessia asks.

"Means they've found a way to use their magic to turn invisible."

"Like the gryphons do," I add.

"Yeah, except it seems the Jersey Devils rely more on being mistaken for ordinary animals," Moss says with excitement. "It's fascinating experiencing them in person. All I want to do is take a bunch of notes."

I bark out a laugh, delighted again by Moss's enthusiasm. "I know that feeling!"

We make it across the Hudson, the dark gray-blue water replaced with crisscrossing streets filled with people and cars. The three Jersey Devils carrying us glide over the High Line, dip and dive between skyscrapers, and zoom up higher into the air. They follow the labyrinthine maze of the city, twisting and turning left and right, until we spy the huge green space of Central Park.

I've been to Central Park a handful of times with Moss and his parents but have never seen it from this view. Usually, we take the train. From all the way up in the sky, all the cyclists and joggers look like ants marching along.

Sinistro buries his head between the Jersey Devil's wings and Alessia's eyes are still shut tight, her lips pressed together in a grim line. Just as we are about one-third of the way over the park, the Jersey Devils take a hard left and careen toward a large light-brick building with two towers. I hold my breath as they head straight for its side, not stopping. At the very last second, the Jersey Devils shoot up in the air, traveling the building's height. It feels impossibly tall—at least fifty stories high. I hold on tighter to the creature's mane and keep another arm around Sinistro.

"Ugh," he moans. "I think I might be sick."

"We'll be there in a second. I'm sure of it."

The Jersey Devils swoop up above the building, their wings flapping steadily, before perching next to a row of angry-looking gargoyles. Alessia stumbles off her Jersey Devil first, hand clutching her stomach while she presses the other against the building's firm facade. She scurries as far from the balcony's railing as possible and takes deep breaths.

"Why couldn't we have landed in Central Park?" she asks.

As I'm getting off my Jersey Devil, I feel his magic pulse against mine as if wanting to communicate. I hold my hand firm to his side as Sinistro hops down and trots over to Alessia, Moss, and Fe. *We brought you straight to the woman who knows where the Streghe del Malocchio's world meets ours. We couldn't drop you off in the park because of a long-standing feud between New York City and New Jersey magical creatures. We do not get along.*

I explain the reason to Alessia and Moss. Alessia scrunches her nose and says, "That's a little silly. A feud?"

I shrug in response and thank the Jersey Devils for their help.

Knock on the glass door. The woman who can help you will be inside.

With that, the Jersey Devils fly off into the sky and what Moss said earlier makes sense. They don't really need to turn invisible because when they're so high up they do kind of look like birds. I sling my backpack over my shoulders and eye the gargoyles whose stony faces now look agitated. Did their expressions change? One of the gargoyles has tiny horns sticking out of its forehead and two pebbly eyes pressed into its face. Another is shorter and squat with only a single eye and a low brow even though it looks like it should have a horn over its head. Then there are two identical gargoyles who have ears that're nearly as big as their wings. They don't *look* like any animals I've ever seen. But it was only an hour or so ago that I first saw a Jersey Devil, so who knows?

We don't have gargoyles in Positano, but there are thousands all over Florence and Rome. There's a rumor that they come alive at night, but I'm not very familiar with gargoyle lore. I do know they're crafted by magical builders for protection. They're extremely loyal to their creators and those who reside in the buildings they guard. I don't know how gargoyles behave, if they're threatening to everyone or just those wishing to harm the people living in their buildings. The hairs on my neck stand up and my stomach flips over.

I'm about to get a closer look when Moss places a hand on my shoulder and asks, "What's the plan?"

"Well, the Jersey Devils said to knock on the balcony's door for the woman who'll help us."

"Seems easy enough," Alessia says with a hint of sarcasm in her tone.

"Are you certain you want to do all of this again?" Sinistro weaves between my legs, his back arched. "Face off against the Streghe del Malocchio?"

"It doesn't seem like we have much of a choice. Just like last time." I shake my head. "Especially if they're stealing creatures and plants."

"But we aren't completely certain, Giada," he says.

"It's the only lead we have."

I march over to the balcony's large glass door and try to peer inside. But the door swirls with silver clouds and I can sense the magic seeping off it like a protective barrier shielding us from seeing in. Carefully, I knock on the door and take a step back. The wind whistles around the balcony. A pigeon coos from its spot atop a gargoyle's head. The faint sounds of honking and car engines drift up to us from down below. But no one stirs behind the door. I knock again, this time for longer. Again, nothing.

"Maybe she's not home?" Moss says, squinting his eyes as if to try and see inside. "Do we want to wait here and see?"

"We're kind of stranded up here until she answers," Alessia adds. "I'd rather be inside. Or on the ground."

"We'd have to whistle for *some* creature's help if we want to get down from here." Moss looks over the balcony's edge and shakes his head. "And who knows if they'll be as easygoing as the Jersey Devils. What if they can smell that I'm from Jersey and refuse to help?"

I knock again, this time banging with the flat side of my fist. After a moment, the door swings open and I fall across the threshold. Alessia helps me up and I tug down my sweater while taking in the room.

We're standing in a penthouse that looks like it's from the 1960s. Frank Sinatra's playing from a huge record player against the wall. The living room is sunken into the floor and faces a huge stone fireplace. Two leopard print couches face one another, wrapped in plastic. Atop a fuzzy white rug that covers the hardwood floors is a turquoise coffee table. The walls are painted flamingo pink. As we walk farther into the penthouse, we spy the kitchen, which has orange cabinets and a lime-green refrigerator and stove. It smells of roses and patchouli; there are vases of flowers on nearly every surface and an incense burner on the fireplace mantel.

"Uhh…hello?" Moss calls out. "Is anybody home?"

"We probably shouldn't be in here alone," Alessia says, her arms wrapped around her torso. "Isn't breaking and entering a felony?"

"We didn't *break* in. I *fell* in," I respond. "Someone must be here if the door just swung open. Doors that are locked don't do that."

"Whatever." Alessia rolls her eyes. "Look. I don't feel comfortable being here without being invited in. Let's just take the elevator to the lobby and maybe ask around down there."

"Oh. You were invited, darling," a low, gruff voice laced with a heavy New York accent says. The five of us whip around, trying to find who the voice belongs to when a dog barks and a puffy Pomeranian bounds toward us. It's a tan ball of fluff with a little red bow in its fur. The Pomeranian circles Sinistro, snuffling all over him. Sinistro glares at the dog before hopping up into my arms.

A woman steps out from behind an acorn door and looks down at us, her hands on her hips. She's tall with broad shoulders and her thick black hair is twisted around gold-plated hair curlers that sit atop her head like a crown. She has tan olive skin and wears a leopard print housecoat that matches her couches, except the spots on her housecoat move around the fabric like a Rorschach test. Her fingers look like claws, lacquered a shiny red that matches her lipstick. Her feet are stuffed into a pair of hot-pink feathered heels. Her whole look is entirely too familiar, and I let out an involuntary groan.

"Ugh. You're a Strega del Malocchio, aren't you?"

The woman scoffs, "An *ex*–Strega del Malocchio. I don't talk to the coven anymore. Name's Angie." It takes me a moment to understand that she said *Malocchio*; she pronounces it like *maloik*. She sticks out a hand for me to shake and I readjust Sinistro so I can take it. Her hand is warm, but I can feel her nails scratch down my wrist. A shiver runs down my spine as I remember the very creepy Madre del Malocchio from Malafi, with her doll-headed cane and horn-shaped hair. "When you become a Strega del Malocchio, you're supposed to give up your name. They move as a unit, ya see." She shrugs, a Cheshire grin curling over her lips. "When I left, I chose a new name for myself."

Woof! Woof! Woof!

"Oh, madone! How rude of me." Angie laughs. "This, my darlings, is Ooh La La."

"You named your dog Ooh La La?" Moss asks, eyebrows knotted together.

"Why wouldn't I? She looks like an Ooh La La, yeah?"

"Uhh… I guess?"

"Madonna mia! We need to get on with it," I shout, my patience snapping like a rubber band. "We need your help, Signorina Angie."

"Oooh! Un'italiana!" Angie coos, as she picks up Ooh La La and leans closer to me and Sinistro. "Are all of ya from the Old Country?"

"Just me and Alessia." I nod over at Alessia, who gives a tiny wave.

"Molto bene!" she says. "I've been to Rome, Florence, Siena, Montalcino, Capri, Positano, and Naples. Beautiful country! Wish I could visit more often."

"That's great, Signorina Angie. We need your hel—"

"Would ya all like tea? Lemonade? Coffee? Milk? Water?" Angie asks as she *click-clacks* on her heels across the parquet floors and into the kitchen. She pulls out a pitcher of pink lemonade and begins pouring into tall glasses with mod-style black cats on them.

"Uh, no. But may I use your bathroom?" Moss asks.

Angie nods to the hallway. "Powder room's second door on the left."

Moss grins and nods in thanks, heading toward the hall.

"Lemonade?" Angie asks again.

"We're not thirsty, but we do have questions about how to find the Streghe del Malocchio."

Angie slams the pitcher down on the counter, pink lemonade sloshing over its sides, and sneers. "I'm not gonna go back there." She makes the sign of the cross with her right hand and kisses her fingers. "Not ever."

"Oh, come on. We can't waste any more time," I begin, but Alessia puts a hand on my arm and shakes her head.

"You don't have to go back to them," Alessia tries, her

voice much gentler than mine. "All we need from you is to show us the entrance."

Angie sighs and steps out of the kitchen with a glass of pink lemonade. She steps down into the living room—the plastic crinkles on the leopard print couch as she sits—and calls for Ooh La La to lie in her lap. Angie gestures for us to do the same and Alessia and I choose the couch opposite hers, the plastic cold as we take our seats.

"I won't step a toe near the entrance to Olde Yorque." Condensation beads on her glass of pink lemonade and she wipes at it with her thumb. "I didn't leave on my own. They kicked me out."

"What?" Alessia exclaims. "Why'd they do that?"

"It wasn't *my* fault, I tell ya. It was a misunderstanding between me and my older sister—she's the Madre of my ex-coven."

"What happened?" Alessia asks politely. I huff next to her, tapping my feet against the bottom of the couch. Alessia swats at my leg and gives me a warning glare.

"We need to hurry up," I whisper through gritted teeth. Time's ticking and we can't spend hours listening to Angie tell us her life story. There's a unicorn and who knows what other magical animals out there that need our help. I can't let them down.

"We need to be nice so she helps us," Alessia replies, her words barely above a breath.

I lean back on the couch and cross my arms as Sinistro purrs in my lap.

"The whole thing was over two hundred years ago, so it feels like ancient history, to me, at least." Angie leaves a red lipstick smudge on the glass when she takes a sip of her pink lemonade. "My sister thought I wanted to steal the throne from her. Ha!" She cackles so hard she begins to cough, and Alessia and I exchange a look. "Anyway. That was nothing but a nasty rumor spread to put a wedge between us. All I ever wanted to do was collect interesting and beautiful magical trinkets. I never wanted to be the Madre. That's a lot of work. But nevertheless." Angie shrugs, a frown tugging at her lips. "I was ousted. I didn't even get to bring my trinkets with me."

Even though I don't want to, I can't help but feel a little bit bad for Angie. Any type of strega or witch can be a Collector—they're a lot like historians of magical artifacts. Most Collectors take the role seriously. From what I know of them, they prefer simple lives and don't want to lead covens.

We sit in silence for a moment, Frank Sinatra's voice drifting on the air. A door creaks open and Moss walks back into the living room, sinking onto the couch next to Alessia and tilting his head back against a fluffy pink throw pillow, shutting his eyes. Fe hops onto the armrest and he runs a finger down her neck. Finally, Angie sighs, "My relationship with my sister was permanently changed for the worst. So, to spite all of them, I moved to the tallest point in the San Remo. As far away from them as I could get at the time. As you can see, my darlings, I never want to be around them ever again."

"No," I blurt before I can stop myself.

Sinistro shoots up and gives me a look. "Giada…" he warns at the same time Angie says, "Excuse me?"

"I said no. I don't accept this."

"Don't accept what?" Angie asks.

"You're taking us to the entrance of Olde Yorque. You have to." Every minute wasted aboveground could mean more trouble for the unicorn.

"I don't gotta do nothing," Angie growls, disturbing Ooh La La on her lap.

"Yes, you do." I put Sinistro on the couch and stand, crossing my arms over my chest. She's just as stubborn as the other Streghe del Malocchio. Just as immovable. An idea crosses my mind and I steel myself to say it. I know what'll get her to help us even though I don't want to do it. "You're no longer a Strega del Malocchio, but you're really no different from them, are you?"

Angie's face reddens and she glares at me. "What do you mean?"

"Let's strike a bargain, shall we?" I say, tapping my foot.

"Giada! Again?" Alessia groans, throwing a hand over her face. "You can't keep making bargains with them."

Angie tilts her head to the side, stroking Ooh La La's fur. "A bargain? Now, I do like those."

"I know you do. You all love bargains. So tell me what it'll cost us."

"If I take you to Olde Yorque's entrance, I'd like you to find my purse for me while you're down there."

"Just a purse?"

"Not *just a purse*. Madone." Angie throws her hands up in the air, rolling her eyes. "My favorite purse. A one-of-a-kind *designer* bag that was made just for me."

My lips curl upward, and I try not to laugh. "What does it look like?"

"It's a brilliant emerald dragon skin with sparkling gold hardware. There are these enchanted gold snakes that slither all around the bag. And the best part is that it's bottomless. Anything and everything fits inside—including many of my favorite trinkets."

"We'll find it for you," I say. "You have my word."

Angie scrunches her nose and sets Ooh La La down on the floor. The little dog toddles over to a gold-plated bowl and takes a long drink of water. "I don't want your word. If you don't hold up your end of the bargain, I want something greater."

Alessia tugs on my hand, but I ignore her and take a deep breath. "What do you want?"

"I collect trinkets, but I also collect different kinds of magic. It looks so pretty, swirling around in crystal glass. I see your familiar. I know you follow Diana, and I don't possess that kind of magic yet." Angie looks at me hungrily and I take a step back, my legs hitting the couch. "I want yours. All of it. Every. Last. Bit."

"Madonna mia. My magic? That's a big request." I stare down at my hands. Her request lands like a slap. Taking another strega's magic is serious. Usually, it's taken involuntarily and is an act of violence—like when the Streghe del Malocchio in Malafi wanted to eat Rocco's heart. Magic can be given over willingly, and the giver can survive, but it doesn't mean it's any less painful. Losing your magic can cause depression. I've read that it feels like a hole has ripped open in your soul and, no matter what you do, it's impossible to fill. When I look back up, Moss is blinking his eyes open, frowning at me.

But I know this in my heart: saving an animal is as important as my magic. Maybe more. Protecting all this world's creatures is what I live for. I can't just turn back now and let the poor unicorn suffer because I'm too scared to make a bargain.

"Well, that's how much I'd rather not go anywhere near Olde Yorque. It's a fair price."

"Giada...you know better than to make deals with the Streghe del Malocchio," Sinistro whispers. "You were lucky it worked out the first time. You might not be so lucky now."

"It'll be okay. I promise," I tell him, even if I don't fully believe it myself. But it *needs* to be okay.

"Do we got a deal or what?" Angie asks. "The entrance to Olde Yorque for my purse. And if I don't get it in forty-eight hours, then I get your magic."

"Yes." I thrust out my hand for Angie to shake.

"Giada!" Moss and Alessia yell at the same time.

Angie takes my hand, a grin curling over her red lips. "Pleasure doing business with you, darling."

I close my eyes, clenching and unclenching my fists. Already it feels like a little bit of my magic has been zapped away even though I know that's not true. We'll rescue the unicorn and find Angie's purse. And if we don't find her purse, giving up my magic to save the unicorn will still be worth it. At least that's what I'm telling myself now.

6

Moss grabs my arm and pulls me near the record player after Angie leaves the living room to go change into a new outfit.

"Are you out of your mind?" Moss asks, his eyes wide.

Alessia joins in at his side, saying, "You can't gamble your magic like this! It's a silly plan. Maybe we should just go back to the Calamoneris' house?"

I shake my head. "It's too late for that now. If I go back on the deal, then my magic's good as gone. We need to go to Olde Yorque, find that unicorn, and get Angie's purse."

"You're in hot water." Sinistro says as he cleans his whiskers, Fe sitting on his head and twittering loudly. Moss looks at the bird and shakes his head, replying with a soft whistle.

"Fe doesn't think this is a good plan."

I snort. "Neither does Sinistro, but what's done is done. I care more about animals than I do my magic. And if the Jersey Devils are right and people are hurting extraordinary animals to create medicine then we need to do something to stop them."

Moss frowns. "What if it's not as bad as the Jersey Devils think?"

"Even if it isn't, we know at least one baby unicorn's been kidnapped for the personal gain of selfish humans, and that's not right."

"But it's worth risking all of your magic? Giada, that's a wild thing to do!"

I narrow my eyes and say between clenched teeth, "Don't you care about the animals being stolen?"

"Of course I care! I care just as much as you do. I never said I didn't!" Moss bites out, his face turning red. "You're just being reckless and stubborn! Who is going to protect *you*?"

"It sounds like you don't—"

"STOP!" Alessia shouts just as the record stops playing.

Angie pops her head out from behind her bedroom door, half her hair bouncing around her shoulders, the other still twisted in gold curlers. "What's all the commotion for?"

I look around the room; even Ooh La La is staring at us like we're some circus sideshow. My face heats up and I try to laugh it off. "Nothing. Just discussing what record to play next."

Angie looks at us for a moment, suspicion etched on her round face, before she nods to the selection of records and says, "Put on Dean," before closing her door once again.

Moss rifles through Angie's collection of records and selects one that has a man in a fedora and brown suit, smiling on the cover. *The Best of Dean Martin* is scrawled across the top. Carefully, Moss pulls out the record and exchanges it with the Frank Sinatra one. A new song begins playing, practically loud enough to rattle the penthouse's windows.

"Who's Dean Martin?" Alessia asks, swaying just a bit to the music.

"You don't know who Dean Martin is?" Moss asks, mouth agape. Alessia shakes her head and Moss grins. "He's only one of the most famous crooners ever. My parents, especially my dad, love him. I do, too. You're lucky you get to discover his music for the first time."

"I like this song," I admit, despite still being kind of mad at Moss.

"It's one of his most famous." Moss clears his throat and begins to sing in a baritone slightly higher than his dad's. He croons about the moon and stars, pizza and pasta e fagioli, and how amore is as wonderful as these things. Magic drifts between his words and this odd inspiration to create, or to dance, or to explore comes over me. It reminds me of when we saw Mrs. Calamoneri in *La Bohème* and her voice sunk between my bones and stirred me to appreciate the beauty of not only the opera's art, but the beauty of all of New York City. Alessia and I join hands and dance around the living room, laughing, as Fe and Sinistro look on. Moss continues singing, his voice in perfect harmony with Dean's.

Alessia and I clap for Moss, whose face turns an even brighter red.

"Bellissimo!" Alessia exclaims. "You're so talented."

"Music's such a huge part of my family and who I am. It makes me happy," he tells Alessia. "It's how my parents show their love, so singing always reminds me of that."

"I didn't know you had your mamma's gift, too," I say. It's interesting that Moss may have a choice when it comes to what he'll specialize in. He may be just as skilled in his mamma's magic. Maybe he has another calling.

Moss smiles shyly and shrugs his shoulders. "I'm just glad my magic's working. At least a little bit."

I place a gentle hand on his arm and grin. "It's a good sign. You're finding your new normal." I look down at my shoes and glance back up quickly. "And I'm sorry for getting mad just now. I know you care about animals as much as me. I'm just stressed out. Thank you for trying to look out for me."

"It's okay," Moss says.

Ooh La La begins yipping just as Angie's bedroom door swings back open to reveal Angie dressed in what looks like an expensive silk blouse with a gold chain print and a leopard print pencil skirt. Her hair is down in big bouncing curls and a pair of oversize diamond encrusted sunglasses sits on her head. She wears hot pink stilettos and on her left wrist is a large gold watch. A ruby encrusted cross hangs from a large gold chain around her neck. Angie snatches Ooh La La up from off the floor and puts her inside a gold designer purse.

"Ready to go, darlings?" Angie asks as she glides over to the kitchen and grabs a set of keys out of a blue glass bowl.

Instead of jumping up and running to the exit the way I want to, I make myself pause and look over to my friends. "Are you ready?" I ask, looking from Alessia to Moss.

"Ready," they say in unison, and I know they would tell

me if they weren't. It's been a long day, and it's not even close to over yet.

Angie ushers us into the elevator and presses the button for the garage. We zoom down in silence as Angie checks her acrylic French manicure for any imperfections. Sinistro rubs against my legs and says, "Just be careful. We've done this before, but I really don't want you to lose your magic. If you do, I won't be your familiar anymore. And we won't be able to talk to each other."

"I hadn't thought of that." I rub his head, thinking of what else I might lose if Angie takes my magic. I wouldn't be able to understand Tartufo, my spider back in Positano, or any other creatures for that matter. I wonder if the people creating all this medicine will put guaritori and magical vets out of work and I won't be healing regardless. I know I'd still miss talking to my animal friends. I take a deep breath as the reality of what I bargained begins to settle in the pit of my stomach like a brick. Tears fill my eyes, but I don't let them fall. It felt like the *right* decision, but it was also rash. "I just wanted so badly to save the unicorn that it didn't matter what I gave up in the moment," I say to Sinistro. "I don't want to lose you—ever. You're a part of my soul. I love you more than anything."

"You've got a big heart…and an even bigger impulsive streak. We'll make things right." He nuzzles into my palm, and I fight the tears pooling in the corners of my eyes. If Sinistro has faith, I need to as well.

The elevator dings and the doors slide open to reveal a huge garage packed with cars of all kinds. Angie steps out first and throws a "Wait here" over her shoulder before disappearing between a minivan and sports car.

A vibrating sound buzzes through the silence and Moss pulls out his phone. He frowns, shaking his head and shoving it back into his pocket. "Mom's blowing up my phone. Turns out they *didn't* sleep all day," he explains, shooting me a look. "She's worried sick. Something bad happening to me is, like, her biggest fear in the entire world. She wants me to come home right now. I don't know what to tell her."

I pull my phone out of my backpack and see a bunch of missed calls and texts from Mrs. Calamoneri. Alessia looks at hers and it's the same from the Pulaskis. Guilt weighs on my shoulders as I think of them all panicking at home while we traipse through the city and get into the exact kind of trouble we shouldn't.

"Do you want to go home?" I ask Moss and Alessia. "I completely get if you want to, but I'm gonna stay."

Moss shakes his head. "No, we've already come this far. I'll tell her we're fine."

"Maybe tell her you wanted to show us your school?" I say. "Would that work?"

"Probably not," Moss says. "But it's something."

"It's better than telling her we're going to see the Streghe del Malocchio." Alessia begins tapping out a text. "I'm letting the Pulaskis know we're going to your school. We can apologize for coming into the city without an adult later. At least they won't come after us now."

"Ugh. My parents are gonna be so mad when we get home. I can't believe I'm doing this," Moss groans as he sends a text to Mrs. Calamoneri before looking at Alessia. "You seemed so levelheaded, but you're as reckless as Giada, you know that?"

Alessia smiles proudly and throws an arm around my shoulder. "I learned from the best."

Moss rolls his eyes and laughs just as a huge neon green 1950s Cadillac convertible screeches to a halt in front of us. On the hood of the car is an evil eye, swiveling and blinking. The steering wheel is white leather, and the seats are covered in leopard print. All the metal detailing is gold. Ooh La La barks from the passenger's side and Angie nods for us all to pile in the back.

We buckle in and I hold Sinistro tight on my lap as Angie peels around a corner and out of the garage onto the busy Manhattan streets. My ponytail whips against my face as the city streets blur together and Angie steers us down-town. I try to focus on what stores and restaurants we're passing to keep track of where we're headed, but Angie's sliding in and out of traffic like a snake. She brakes fast and maneuvers behind screeching trucks and taxis, then shifts gears and zips ahead of honking cars, cutting them off. I dig my hand into the upholstery and make the sign of the cross for protection. I thought Rocco was a bad driver when he was learning how to handle Positano's steep curves, but Angie is way worse.

"I feel like I might hack up a hair ball," Sinistro com-plains. His eyes are closed shut and he lets out an ear-piercing yowl.

"Can you wait until we're out of the car and you're not sitting in my lap?" I ask, feeling my own belly gurgling in revolt.

I glance over at Alessia, Moss, and Fe to see that they all look to be varying shades of green as well. At least Sinistro and I wouldn't be the only ones puking in Angie's fancy car. But just as I'm about to lean over the convertible's side to throw up, we come to a screeching halt outside of a restaurant sitting on what looks to be the intersection of Chinatown and Little Italy. *Signora Zhao's* is scrawled in fancy white letters on the window.

"Is this it?" Alessia asks, quickly unbuckling and leaping

out of the car onto solid ground. Moss, Sinistro, Fe, and I follow right after her and I practically kiss the sidewalk out of relief.

"Not quite." Angie snatches up Ooh La La and scoots out of the car.

"Huh. They serve spaghetti *and* dumplings," I say, as Alessia and I inspect the tattered menu sitting on a stand just outside Signora Zhao's. My stomach starts to rumble. I could go for both right now. "That's interesting." I turn to Moss and raise an eyebrow. "Why's that, you think?"

"Probably because Chinatown got bigger while Little Italy shrunk. The reason they're so close to each other is because back then, Italian Americans were one of the only groups renting and selling to Chinese Americans. We're right on the border between the two neighborhoods and both have changed so much over the years."

"Wow. And so we have spaghetti and dumplings."

"Exactly."

"Darlings! You're gonna go this way." Angie nods her chin in the direction of a sidewalk grate.

"Wait." Alessia scrunches her nose. "All the way down there?"

"It's *one* of the ways into the city. Probably the easiest one to get to."

I march up to the grate and toe it with my boot. "Are you gonna get any closer?" I ask Angie from over my shoulder.

"Absolutely not. I prefer staying on the Chinatown side of the street, thank you very much."

"It's just a black pit down there." Moss crouches next to the grate and shines his phone's light into the darkness. "It goes on forever."

"Well, I guess we'll just have to jump and see for ourselves what's on the other side," I say.

"Ugh. I can already feel last night's dinner rising into my throat," Alessia groans.

"We need to do it for the unicorn. Come on!" I get on my knees and unlatch the grate, yanking it hard off the hole. Moss and Alessia hurry to the opposite side and help me pull it up. The grate creaks and scrapes against the sidewalk, but after a few minutes of struggle, it's pushed against the side of Signora Zhao's.

"Uhh…darlings?" Angie calls from a few feet away. She's petting Ooh La La's head and a smile curls over her lips. "Don't forget our little bargain."

"Yeah, yeah, yeah," I say. "Creepy dragon skin purse with gold slithery snakes."

"And if you don't get my purse…I get your magic."

I swallow hard, clutching the grate to still my shaking.

"We'll find her purse," Alessia whispers. "I promise."

"Yeah, we don't have a choice," Moss adds.

I swallow hard and the brick in my stomach flips over. *Remember the unicorn and the other creatures you'll save*, I think. I give Angie a wave before staring down into the abyss that is the entrance to Olde Yorque. Carefully, I swing my legs over into the hole. Sinistro climbs into my arms, and I hold him tight.

"Are you ready?" I breathe. "To do this again?"

"Ready as I'll ever be, I suppose," Sinistro says.

"On the count of three?"

"One…" Sinistro says as I scoot my behind farther off the sidewalk's edge. A warm wind picks up from the hole and the smell of fresh tomato sauce swirls around us.

"Two…" I say, squeezing Sinistro tighter to still my shaking hands. Sweat beads on the back of my neck and dots my brow. My mouth's drier than a piece of stale bread. On the wind, the faint sound of screeching violins drifts toward us and I can already feel the headache pounding at the front of my skull.

"Three…" Sinistro and I say at the same time. With a final breath, I push off the sidewalk and fall into the nothingness. Down, down, down toward Olde Yorque.

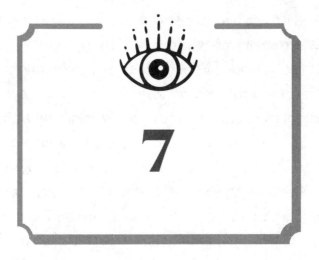

7

Wind whips in my ears and swirls around my ponytail. I hold on to Sinistro with all my strength as we tumble down through the darkness. The violins scratch against my skull and they sound just like the ones that played endlessly in Malafi—totally obnoxious. Hopefully those horrible crows don't show up next. My heart's in my throat as we zoom farther and farther into the center of the earth, way below New York City.

But then the free fall stops. We begin to float down gently like a feather on a summer's breeze. The violins fade out and instead Dean Martin's unforgettable voice croons around us. And that delicious scent of tomato sauce comes back.

"This isn't so bad," Sinistro says.

"We've dealt with worse."

A faint light appears beneath us and grows brighter as we get closer to the ground. In the blink of an eye, the darkness fades and below us is a sprawling city with millions of fairy lights strung up on the brick walls. We land gently on our feet in the middle of a bustling subway station filled with Streghe del Malocchio too busy coming and going to notice me. It's weird. I'm used to getting mean stares from them—at least from the ones in Malafi. But these streghe don't even give me a passing glance as they hurry about.

Trains cut through the air, flying in every direction instead of sticking to any kind of track. Above us is a sky made of asphalt, also covered in fairy lights, that's dotted with holes like the one we fell through. Dean Martin continues to play all throughout the city, his voice echoing off the buildings. Instead of the trulli in Malafi—those squat, white houses with huge roofs decorated with symbols—gigantic, spindly brick apartment buildings crowd nearly every available space. Laundry is strung up between them. Streghe del Malocchio sit on their fire escapes, drinking wine and shouting to one another from across the way.

"Whoa! That was wild," I hear Moss say over my shoulder. I spin around to see Moss and Fe just behind me and

Sinistro. Alessia drifts down a moment later and shakes out her short curls.

"I was scared for a moment there. Madonna mia, my stomach almost flew out of my mouth." Alessia laughs, holding tight to her cornicello. "But then it was pretty nice."

"Look at this place!" I shout, jumping up on my toes. "It's so different from Malafi, but somehow still the same?"

Alessia and Moss assess Olde Yorque, their mouths agape as they take in the flying subway trains and strange asphalt sky.

I nudge Moss in the side and can't help but grin as I say, "Told you so! They really do exist."

Moss rolls his eyes, but a smile curls over his lips, too.

"Did you see the scales, Giada?" Alessia asks, pointing to the lone skyscraper miles away from us. It's a chrome monster and at its tippy top is a silver lady draped in a long silver gown with her arms outstretched, a plate dangling from each hand. Weighing down the plates are twin spheres filled with cloudy light. From here, they appear balanced. I breathe a sigh of relief. No good can come from those scales being out of whack.

"That must be where the Madre del Malocchio lives."

"We should head straight to her, then, right?" Alessia asks.

Moss shakes his head. "It's probably better to get some

information first. We need details about the missing unicorn and where Angie's purse may be." He stifles a yawn, pulling out his water bottle to take a sip. "Let's chat up the others and see what we can find out *before* we go to their leader."

"Good idea," I say. "Let's take the subway. We can ask questions there." We push our way through the throng of streghe hurrying about the station until we reach the platform. There's no street name or sign like on a normal platform. But there are what look like sparkling runes suspended several feet above us. They flash red before shifting positions, dancing in the air like fairies. Upon closer inspection, it looks like they *are* fairies. Several tiny ones, flitting about and changing positions to form runes.

"I've never actually seen fairies before," Moss breathes. "I've only read about them."

"Their wings are important in love and friendship potions. Even some protection potions, too." I frown up at the herd of fairies as they rearrange themselves once again. They don't look unhappy or trapped down here. In fact, they're squeaking to one another and moving with grace. It looks like the Streghe del Malocchio on the subway platform even respect them, staring up at them with reverence. No one's trying to lure them down to yank off their wings like I'd expect—considering we're on the hunt for folks stealing magical creatures.

"Look!" Alessia shouts. "A train's flying in."

I tear my eyes away from the fairies to see a shiny gold subway train flying fast into the station. The herd of fairies zip away in a brilliant ruby cloud just as the train whips through. At the very last second, the train comes to a sudden halt.

Dozens and dozens of Streghe del Malocchio file out in a never-ending line. Some are tall, while others are short. Some wear huge hats that knock into other streghe and others have their hair piled high in intricate braids, curls, and knots. But the thing that makes them all so alike is that every single one is dressed in high fashion, just like the streghe in Malafi. This time, headed to New York Fashion Week instead of Milan.

Finally, all the Streghe del Malocchio have exited the train and the sea of streghe waiting on the platform crush their way through the sliding doors. Like fish in the middle of the school, we go with the flow of the group, piling into the train until we're pressed between a metal pole and a row of seated streghe.

"Agh! Your elbow's in my back," Moss groans.

"Your back's in my elbow," Alessia protests.

"Both of you need to get your feet off my feet," I huff.

"That's not my foot," Moss and Alessia growl in unison.

I look down to see Sinistro and Fe both planted on my feet. Fe flaps up between the three of us and lands on Moss's head. Sinistro claws up my jeans and into my arms.

"My goodness, it's hard to breathe in here," Sinistro complains.

"You're telling me."

The sliding doors close with a *ding-dong* and a tinny voice announces something through the speakers in the train. "Next stop…"

"What did she say?" Alessia asks. "I didn't catch it."

"Me neither," Moss says, brows furrowed. "Are the streets named the same as they are above?"

I shrug. "Beats me."

The train takes off and glides easily through the air at a breakneck speed. Outside the window, buildings and lights blur together. I grip Sinistro under my arm and hold on to the pole for dear life. We dive underneath a bridge and coil around an apartment building like an anaconda before shooting off until we hit the asphalt sky and dip back down.

Alessia has her eyes closed and is muttering what I think is a protection spell under her breath. Finally, we reach another station, and the doors open once more. Some streghe exit and new ones come on. I nudge Moss as the doors close again and the muffled voice announces our next stop. "We need to start asking around," I whisper. "Let's ask about the unicorn first. Ease our way into questions about the purse."

"But you can't save the unicorn if you don't have your magic," Alessia reasons, groaning slightly as the train jerks abruptly. "Purse first, unicorn second."

Moss nods and taps her on the shoulder, motioning to move toward the front of the train car. Alessia shakes her head and wraps her arms around the pole tighter, saying, "Go on without me. I'm feeling queasy again."

Moss, Fe, Sinistro, and I squeeze between streghe and walk all the way to the back of the train. "Let's start here and work our way to the front," Moss says. "But we need to be discreet."

"Discreet." I roll my eyes. "I don't do discreet."

"Ugh. You're impossible."

I spy a strega in a lime-green leather pencil skirt and pink frilly blouse and sky-high black stilettos. Her platinum blond hair is braided into a giant bow on the top of her head and her lips are painted a bright purple that complements her light olive skin. She has her legs crossed and a newspaper splayed on her lap. Bold block runes flash across the newspaper's front and shift in size and shape as she reads.

"Umm…" I stand in front of her. She looks up sharply, her dark eyes narrow, and purses her lips as if waiting for me to continue. I clear my throat and say, "Hi… I'm Giada Bellantuono and this is my friend Massimo Calamoneri, but he goes by Moss."

The strega blinks up at us, fiddling with the gold *M* earring in her right ear.

"Okay. Well, we wanted to know if you knew anything about a purse that belonged to the Madre's sister? The one who was kicked out of Olde Yorque?"

She arches a perfectly sculpted eyebrow, but still says nothing. I take a step back and bump into Moss, who's shaking his head. "I told you we should've been discreet," he whispers in my ear. "Charging in and being direct isn't going to get us answers. These ladies clearly don't want to talk to us."

"Fine. Let's try your way."

We push through the crowd and find another strega wearing a black sheath dress, leather gloves, and gray pumps. Her black hair is pin straight—a sharp contrast to her pale white skin—and on top of her head is a black feathered fascinator with a black net covering her face. She frowns at me and Moss before turning to stare out the window.

I press Moss forward and nod for him to ask her the

questions. Moss takes a deep breath and forces a smile onto his face before saying, "Hello. Lovely day, isn't it?"

The strega scrunches her nose. "I wouldn't know... I haven't been aboveground in centuries."

"Oh. Yeah, that makes sense I guess." Moss scratches the back of his neck. Fe tweets in his ear and he shakes his head. "Olde Yorque's a beautiful city. I love all the... erm..." he looks around the subway car for support "...the ambiance is nice. In New York City, the subways have fluorescent lights. The soft lighting in here is much nicer."

"Of course it's nicer," the strega snaps. "We *perfected* the subway system."

"Of course! Who'd want to live up above anyway? You've got so much down here."

"We sure do. Whoever would want to live in that terrible *new* city—with its extravagant stage shows, thousands of unique restaurants, and parks full of flowers—is truly ridiculous."

"I couldn't agree more. No one wants those things."

I look down at the ground and can't help but roll my eyes.

"Quite the charmer," Sinistro says.

"Speaking of not wanting to live in New York City... I heard about a Strega del Malocchio who was forced out of Olde Yorque and had to live up there. Sounds awful."

The strega looks down at us and sneers. "What're you after?"

Moss glances at me and I nod for him to keep pressing. He sighs and continues, "I just heard a rumor is all. About the Madre's sister and her special designer purse."

"Get out of my sight," the strega snaps. "Now!"

Moss and I hurry away and regroup a few feet down. "These witches are as scary as the stories make them out to be," Moss says.

"Like I said before—told you so!"

"Yeah, yeah, yeah."

"Actually, this behavior's tame." I shake my head, eyeing the other streghe on the train who are now starting to pay closer attention to us. My gaze slides over to Alessia, who's still hugging the pole, face scrunched in worry, and relief washes over me. She's safe from the streghe. At least for now. "We need to keep asking around."

"I don't know if that's a good idea anymore."

"Come on, Moss. We have to find that purse. And we haven't even gotten to questions about the unicorn yet."

Moss sighs and twists one of his curls between his fingers. "Just one more witch. If it doesn't work, then let's just go to the Madre's place and ask her."

"Deal."

I grab Moss by the hand and drag him over to a nice-looking older strega with deep olive skin and short silver hair tucked into a crown made from pink daisies. She's wearing a flowing emerald dress covered in yellow feathers. On her feet is a pair of brown boots. She grins at us and reveals a set of sharp-looking teeth. I swallow my nerves and grin back, giving her a tiny wave.

"Ciao! I'm Giada Bella—"

The strega cuts me off with a laugh. "Oh, I know who you are."

"You do?" My eyebrows knot together, and my lips tug downward.

"News travels fast between covens, sweetheart."

"Ah. Hopefully it's all good news," I say with a feeble laugh.

The strega's grin broadens and I squeeze Sinistro closer to my chest, gripping Moss's hand tighter.

"I've watched you march all over this train, bothering other streghe with your questions about the Madre's sister."

"We didn't mean to be a bother," Moss chimes in. The strega just waves her hand as if it's a nonissue.

"Someone like you doesn't need to waste time pestering the rest of us." The strega stands and places her wrinkled hands on our shoulders.

"Hey! Let go of us!" I yell, trying to wriggle free from her surprisingly strong grip.

"You should go right to the source of truth," she says. "To the Madre herself."

"Giada! Moss!" Alessia shoves through the crowd and almost reaches us when the strega in black yanks her back by the arm. "Ouch! Get off me!"

"Here's another one to bring to the Madre!" the strega in black bellows and pulls Alessia after her. She pushes her next to Moss and me just as a circle of streghe begin to form around us.

"To the Madre you'll go. She'll deal with you all," the gray-haired strega proclaims.

The circle of streghe begin to chant, their voices hushed and scratchy like an ill-fitting sweater. I begin to sweat, feeling the nerves building in my stomach and shooting out all over my body. Suddenly, the lights in the train go dark and we come to a jarring halt. Moss, Fe, and Alessia tumble into Sinistro and me, nearly knocking us over. But as soon as the train stops, it zooms off again in the opposite direction.

"What's going on?" Alessia whispers.

"We're taking you to the Madre, sweetheart," the gray-haired strega says. "All will be sorted soon."

The streghe continue to chant as Olde Yorque flashes by in reverse outside the window. We take a sharp turn and all of a sudden the single chrome skyscraper we saw earlier emerges out from the brick buildings like a splinter in a thumb. The woman standing at its top with the scales grows closer with each second. Soon I can make out her eyes and I notice how they follow us, tracking the train's every movement as if she were alive and not made of metal. I take a deep breath, focusing on the magic at my core, calling upon it just in case things take a turn for the worse. Just in case this Madre wants trouble.

8

The Madre del Malocchio's penthouse is larger than Angie's but just as tacky. The walls and floors are white marble and cold, reminding me of a supervillain's fortress cut into some icy cavern. A fresco depicting moving clouds and a gigantic blossoming olive tree covers the ceiling. The fresco shifts from sunrise to day to sunset to night over the span of a few minutes. At the ceiling's center is a gold-and-crystal chandelier. It's so big it nearly knocks into the peacock feather and sunflower arrangement sitting in a giant gold vase atop the gold table in the middle of the penthouse's entryway. The sunflowers' heads tilt back and forth, some leaning into each other as if in hushed conversation, others craning like they're trying to get a closer look at us.

It's all *a lot*.

I look over my shoulder at the only obvious exit—two gold doors pressed into the white marble like chocolate chips in cookie dough. A trio of streghe stare down at us, blocking the way out. They snatched us right off the train as soon as it pulled into the subway station and carted us off to an express elevator that sped all the way up to the penthouse. Alessia turned white as a ghost and looked like she was about to vomit all over her shoes. I was too angry to give these streghe the satisfaction of seeing me nauseous.

The three streghe shove us farther into the penthouse and into a marble covered sitting room that has floor-to-ceiling windows overlooking the rest of Olde Yorque. An ornate rug covers the floors, and the sofas are gold with a heavy green velvet upholstery. The room smells like lemons and fresh linen. I'd expect fire and brimstone for the Madre's lair, not cleaning supplies.

"Ah! How intriguing," a voice booms around the sitting room. A set of black marble stairs unfurls from the ceiling like a vulture's wings. On them is a tiny woman with yellow curls that fan from her head like a sunflower's petals. Two round splotches of blush coat her pale olive face, and pink gloss shines on her lips. She wears a yellow silk corset, and a green tulle skirt juts out at her hips and falls like a ballerina's tutu. On her feet are a pair of green stilettos that lace up her legs in ribbons. She looks just like the sunflowers in her entryway, and I think of the fields of sunflowers in Toscana. Maybe that's where she got her inspiration.

"The Bewildering Bellantuono." She hops down the last step onto the floor and the stairs retract up into the ceiling behind her. A grin curls over her lips, exposing a smear of pink lipstick on her teeth. "To what do the Streghe del Malocchio of Olde Yorque owe the pleasure?"

"Uhh…" I arch an eyebrow, noticing that she pronounces *Malocchio* just like Angie did. "Bewildering? I don't know about that."

"That's what my sisters in Malafi call you." Her grin widens as she crosses to the center of the room and does a little twirl, her tutu fanning through the air. "But they're rather silly, aren't they? Such old customs. And so much superstition."

"I thought all Streghe del Malocchio were superstitious?" Alessia asks, her voice barely above a whisper.

Madre shrugs. "To varying degrees. We live in the United States, honey. In the greatest city in the world. We're not as old-fashioned."

The trio of streghe standing behind us chuckle.

I narrow my eyes. An odd feeling of loyalty flutters in my chest. It's one thing for *me* to laugh at the Malafi streghe about their old-school ways, but *these* streghe can't. "Hey, they aren't that old-fashioned. They just like tradition is all."

But Madre ignores me.

"Now." She taps a long, neon yellow nail on her chin and tilts her head. "Why are you here?"

"Well, we're here for a couple reasons." I glance between Moss and Alessia, who both nod for me to continue. For some reason, this Madre's behavior—her calmness and humor—have thrown me for a loop and make me more nervous than Malafi's cold and direct Madre did. "The main one being we're looking for a unicorn that went missing from Teterboro Airport." I cross my arms over my chest and plant my feet firmer on the floor, trying to muster all my confidence. Doubt scratches at the walls of my mind, but I brush it away. I didn't come this far to be wrong. I just know they're in on this. "We have reason to believe you've got something to do with it."

Madre stands taller, her grin turning sour. "A unicorn? You believe we'd take a unicorn? Madone." Confused whispers erupt behind us as the trio of streghe speak among themselves. Madre snaps her fingers and the whispers

119

are cut off, the room descending into silence. "We would never do such a thing, honey."

"We found six pennies, tail sides up." Moss digs in his pocket and produces the pennies, glimmering in his palm. "A sign of bad luck."

Madre approaches us, her sunflower hair casting a shadow on our faces. She snatches the pennies from Moss's hand and brings them close to her eyes for inspection. "How interesting. I'll admit this kind of looks like our handiwork." She laughs to herself, a light trilling noise that echoes around the room. "But it isn't us. We may be a lot of things, honey, but we'd never be so tacky."

My shoulders slump, but I stand firm. "How do I know you're not lying?"

"If we had your unicorn, you'd know. We never hide our true intentions."

I think back to the Madre in Malafi, and how she was up-front about what they would do to Rocco if I didn't bring them their night sky. But then I remember what happened with Papa Gryphon—how a few renegade Streghe del Malocchio tried to take him—and an idea strikes me.

"What if one of your coven's working alone?" I look back at the three streghe before whipping around to face Madre once more. Desperation laces through my words as I add, "I mean, that's totally possible, right?"

Madre clasps her hands in front of her. "I'm sorry, honey, but it isn't us. I do think I know who's behind it, though."

"Wait. For real?" Moss asks. "Why didn't you lead with that?"

"I was working my way to it," Madre says. "And I'm frankly horrified that this has happened." Her eyes turn flinty as she presses her lips into a firm line. "Someone has framed us. Used our reputation against us since we refused to help them."

"Well...who is it?" Alessia shakes her head. "Who'd do such a thing?"

"An organization with a keen interest in exploiting magical creatures for their own gain. When they came to us with their proposition, I gave them a flat no," Madre explains. "Helping them with their scheme would throw *everything* out of balance. The ramifications would be cataclysmic."

"What did they want you to do?" Moss asks.

Madre hesitates for a moment before saying, "I cannot say. As Streghe del Malocchio, we must maintain balance and remain neutral in our dealings. Having a hand in their plot would cause a major shift in the scales. It could cause this world's magic to become unstable." She frowns, twisting a gold ring around her left thumb. "Which is incredibly dangerous. Unstable magic could not only reveal the

Streghe del Malocchio to the world, which we certainly do *not* want, but could put our coven's and other streghe's magic in jeopardy. And now this organization is framing us. Of course they are." Madre scoffs and tosses her hands in the air. "It's easy to blame us because we're already seen as monsters by other streghe."

"Madre, who came to you with this plan? Who's stealing all these magical creatures?" I ask.

Madre tilts her head to the side, her curls tickling her shoulder. She raises her perfectly plucked eyebrows but doesn't say anything. "I've already said too much. *Telling* you exactly who is doing this isn't our place either. But I can tell you that we won't stand in your way if you continue to pursue these individuals."

I stare at Madre, heat rising to my face. Of course this is her response. The Streghe del Malocchio generally stay out of what's going on up above them unless the scales are threatened. If they believe the scales will shift if they *do* help, then they'll absolutely stay out of it.

"Ugh! This is a load of nonsense!" I slam my foot on the marble floor and immediately regret it when a sharp pain shoots up my leg.

"Sorry, honey, but my hands are tied."

"Whatever. We'll figure it all out on our own, no thanks to you and the rest of the Streghe del Malocchio."

"What about the purse?" Alessia whispers, putting a hand on my arm. She speaks louder, eyes moving to the Madre, and says, "We're also looking for a special purse. You might know it?"

Madre arches an eyebrow at Alessia, and she continues, "Well, it's emerald dragon skin with gold hardware and—"

"And gold snakes that wriggle all over it?" Madre slithers her hand through the air, her jaw set and shoulder straight. "I don't know what you're talking about."

"But you just described what it looks like?" Alessia protests. "Madonna mia. I'm not going to beat around the bush. It belonged to your sister."

The three streghe behind us gasp and their whispers begin once more. Madre snaps her fingers and the sound bounces off the walls. The streghe immediately go silent.

"I don't have a sister," she says, her voice colder than all the marble in her penthouse. "It's time you three leave."

And with that, the Madre clicks her heels together and the large staircase unfolds from the ceiling once more. She glides up the stairs, disappearing without another word or glance in our direction.

"Well, that was a colossal waste of time," Moss complains once we're back on the train and headed the way we originally came. Or at least I think we are—it's hard to tell when the train's not on a track. "We could've stayed home with my parents and the Pulaskis and figured it all out together. Would've saved ourselves a whole lot of grief from my mom. We're going to be in so much trouble when we get back."

We stand squished together among the Streghe del Malocchio who ignore us and go about their days. It's hot in the train and the ever-present smell of tomato sauce is starting to make me sick. Alessia is taking deep breaths through her nose and is gripping the pole, knuckles white. Ugh. We need to get out of here and up to New York City.

"We aren't going back yet," I say.

"Do you have a plan B?" Moss asks.

I shake my head. "Not yet, but I don't think going home is gonna help us. I don't think the unicorn's in New Jersey."

"And the Pulaskis checked with Vince," Moss says. "He said he doesn't think anyone else would've flown off with the unicorn."

"It just makes sense that the unicorn's in New York City. It's the biggest city in the world! The Jersey Devils said other magical creatures in the area are going missing. Plenty of magical creatures call New York City their home—you know that better than any of us, Moss. Plus, a base of operations in this city means easy access to other places nearby, like New Jersey and Connecticut. Whoever's taking these creatures isn't going anywhere far away. I think they're sticking around. Just out of sight."

Sinistro pats me on the shoulder and says, "Giada, someone's watching us."

"What're you talking about?" I crane my neck around to get a better look at the streghe nearby, but none of them look interested in what Moss and I are discussing. In fact, most of them are doing everything they can to avoid eye contact with us. Obviously, the Madre's declaration that we need to leave as soon as possible traveled fast.

Fe says something to Moss, who also starts looking around the train. He shrugs his shoulders and turns back to me, saying, "Anyway, I think we need to regroup. I need to be near a bathroom if we're going to keep at this, and I'll need some *actual* rest. Honestly, you both look like you could use some, too. Maybe we can go to my school and do some research in the library. Madre called it an *organization*. Meaning it's not just one person. So we know we're looking for an organization that's using extraordinary creatures and plants to create medicine."

"Yeah, but they're *destroying* creatures and plants. Draining their resources."

"Right."

The train comes to a rough stop, making me topple into Moss and Fe while Alessia trips over herself in her efforts to get off the train as fast as possible. We follow her and take in the platform. It *looks* like the platform we landed on when we jumped down the hole to Olde Yorque. But who really knows? They all look pretty similar. A few feet away are four ladders—one yellow, one green, one violet, and one pink. They climb up the side of the brick wall and up, up, up into the darkness. Next to each ladder is a bronze sign emblazoned with a street name: Mulberry Street, West 51st Street, 125th Street, and Avenue B.

"This must be a way out," I say. "Let's get climbing."

Alessia looks up at the ladders and shakes her head. "I don't think I'm going with you."

"What?" I follow her gaze and put an arm around her shoulders. "It'll be okay. I know it's high up, but there's no other way for us to get out of here. At least not that I'm aware of."

"It's not the height." Alessia gives me a small smile. "We still need to get Angie's purse, Giada. You need your magic."

I drop my arm and frown at Alessia. "You're staying down here? To look for Angie's purse?"

"One of us needs to." Alessia squeezes my hand. "I don't want you losing your magic because of some bargain that didn't even pan out for us."

Tears form in my eyes and I wrap Alessia in a huge hug,

nearly knocking her over. "Are you sure? I don't want you down here with the Streghe del Malocchio. What if they kidnap you like last time?"

Alessia laughs. "They don't have a reason to this time. At least not yet. And we know them—I'm sure they'll send you some sign of bad luck if they decide to kidnap me, so you'll know if I'm in trouble."

"You seem pretty calm about all this."

Alessia pulls out of our hug and shrugs. "It's like Moss said—someone's got to look out for you while you're looking out for all the animals. You're my best friend. *And* you saved my life last year. Of course I'm going to help you."

"Ti voglio bene, Alessia." The tears fall down my cheeks and I wipe them away with the back of my hand.

"I love you, too. And if you don't hear from me before Angie's two days are up, well, you know where to find me."

Alessia gives me one last hug and scritches Sinistro on the chin. She nods to Moss and Fe before hurrying back over to the subway platform and hopping onto the train just before its doors close.

I take a deep breath and turn to Moss, saying, "I'm just worried about her. The last time I dragged her into a mess with the Streghe del Malocchio, she ended up in a cage next to my brother."

"She knows what she's doing, Giada. Alessia's brave," he reassures me.

"I know. Thanks." I wipe the last of the tears away and give Moss a tight smile. "Let's get out of here."

"West Fifty-First is closest to my school."

"Perfect." I eye the green ladder and grasp the first rung.

"Hey!" A little voice calls over the Dean Martin music. I pause and look around, trying to find its source. "Hey there! Yeah, I'm talking to you."

Finally, I look down and see a girl a couple years younger than us. She's short with bright blond curls, big green eyes, and freckles that cover her pale face. She wears a lilac dress with white boots and a white witch's hat with a brim that's just a touch too big. The girl looks *entirely* out of place in Olde Yorque.

"She's the one I saw watching us on the train," Sinistro says just as the girl sticks out her hand for me to shake.

"Who're you?" I ask, taking her hand and shaking it before Moss does the same.

"Name's Jodi. I'm here to help you."

I blink at the girl a few times and tilt my head to the side in confusion. "Uhh. What?"

"My name's Jodi and I want to help you," she says, slower this time.

"I'm Giada and he's Moss," I say. "What're you doing down here?"

She laughs and says, "I should be the one asking you that, but I already know. I'm a Strega del Malocchio in training."

"But you have a name?" Moss asks, brows knotted. "Don't Streghe del Malocchio not have names?"

"In training," she repeats, shaking her head. "I don't give up my name until I turn thirteen!"

"Oh, well, Jodi. It was nice meeting you, but we gotta be on our way," I explain.

"You seem to be forgetting that I offered my help. The Madre's my mentor. She told me to follow you three and make sure you left. But before that I overheard your conversation." Jodi frowns and stares between Moss and me. "Hearing about all these helpless creatures being taken almost made me cry. It's terrible. I never want to see anyone or anything being harmed."

"Why do you want to help us?" I narrow my eyes at her, suspicious of any Strega del Malocchio who would offer help. Even if she technically isn't one yet. "What's in it for you?"

Moss nudges me in the ribs and throws me a glare before saying, "What my rude friend is trying to ask is what kind of bargain do we need to make? Since Streghe del Malocchio like bargains."

"Oh! Well, no bargain. I just want to help. You have my word." Jodi giggles and tosses her curls back over her shoulders.

"No bargain?" I scoff. "I don't know about that."

Moss ignores me and says, "We're currently starting from scratch. Your Madre was of absolutely no help to us."

"Hmm. I don't think we'll be starting over. Since I'm technically not a full Strega del Malocchio yet, I think I can be of assistance." Jodi digs through the seafoam green beaded bag hanging from her shoulder and produces a small business card. "I found this."

She hands it over to me and Moss reads over my shoulder. It's a gold-rimmed card with a merry-go-round stamped on its front and the name Joe Lombardo underneath it. On the back is the number seventeen. It glows under the fairy lights.

"What does this mean?" I ask.

"It's a lead, of course. I was shadowing the Madre the day a strange man came to her asking for help. He said he worked for an organization that wanted the Madre to convince every other Streghe del Malocchio coven to kidnap the magical creatures in their regions. She said, *not a chance*, because of the scales, like she told you." Jodi wiggles her fingers through the air. "I think he's who you might be looking for. He also mentioned the stables in Central Park."

I flip the card over again and stare at the merry-go-round. "Where'd you get this?"

Jodi giggles again. "Oh, you know. I'm really good at tracking and stealing things. Blending in is another specialty. My mom says it's because of my magic." She shrugs and smiles brightly. "I took it from the Madre's foyer after she told me to follow you. She just left it out in the open by her vase of sunflowers. I noticed it right away. It was practically begging to be stolen."

"That's awfully convenient." I cross my arms over my chest, my gaze fixed on Jodi. "Are you sure she didn't leave it out on purpose? Is this all some weird trick you're playing with the Madre?"

"I wouldn't play a trick like this," Jodi says, her eyes wide.

"But the Madre might." I arch an eyebrow.

"Anyway!" Moss says, pushing through my skepticism. "Do you really think you can help us?"

"I know I can. And I'll prove it to you right now—I heard you say you needed a bathroom?"

Moss and I look at each other skeptically.

"Yeah…?" he says.

"There's a public one down the platform, a little past

the Avenue B ladder. Don't worry, public bathrooms in Olde Yorque are kept spotless, unlike their counterparts aboveground. We actually care about the well-being of our citizens here," she says, crossing her arms in front of her chest.

"Moss, I don't trust—" I try to grab his arm, but he's already walking past the ladders, weaving through streghe as Fe flies above him, and sure enough, within a few seconds I hear him call: *"She's right! I'll be right back!"*

Jodi raises her eyebrows at me, a pleased grin spreading across her face.

"And you're allowed up in New York City?" I ask, ignoring her.

"I live up there until I'm officially a Strega del Malocchio," she explains. I raise an eyebrow. "Are you sure about this? About helping us without any kind of deal in place?"

"I just want to make sure the animals are okay," she says, then gestures behind us, back into Olde Yorque. "I don't have to play by their rules."

"I don't know why, but I think we can trust her," Sinistro says, and I crouch down to scritch him between his ears. "She did just help Moss, after all."

"Thanks for giving Moss a heads-up about the bathrooms," I say reluctantly, standing back up.

"When you gotta go, you gotta go!" Jodi says, chuckling.

A train comes and goes and Jodi and I fidget beside each other in awkward silence for a few more minutes before Moss and Fe return.

"Alright! Thanks for that, Jodi. Let's go!" Moss says, clapping his hands together. "If we're going to the stables near Central Park first, we'll still want to take the green ladder."

Moss begins to climb up the tall ladder.

I plaster a smile on my face. I'm still unsure about Jodi. But we need her help. We don't have any other leads. I carefully grab onto the ladder. "Welcome to the team, Jodi," I say. And with that, I begin the long climb back up to New York City.

9

The horse stable isn't at all what I imagined. For one, I thought it'd be like the stables in Italy. Fresh hay, plenty of food and water, clean stalls, and grassy space outside for them to frolic. Instead, the stable is on the outskirts of Central Park near Columbus Circle, situated among apartment and office buildings, and right next to a noisy, busy road that reeks of gasoline and garbage. An old wooden sign that reads Big Apple Horses hangs from rusted, creaking chains over a pair of equally rusted doors.

I push one of the doors open and am hit with a wall of hot, humid air. Inside it smells like the stalls have never been mucked out. There are too many horses shoved to-gether, like rivets on the side of a ship.

"Hello?" I call into the stable. Jodi walks ahead of me down the row of stalls and makes a left down a narrow-looking hall.

"I'm going to do some investigating," she calls over her shoulder before disappearing.

"What could she be investigating without us?" I whis-per to Moss. "You should follow her."

"I'm not gonna *follow* her. Especially if we want her to trust us."

"Trust is a two-way street," I say. "*We* need to trust *her*, too."

"You're being silly."

"I'm being practical." But I walk past Moss and yell, "Hello? Anyone in here?" Flies bob up and down, circling the horses' rear ends and giant piles of horse poop. Their buzzing and the muffled noises from the street are the only sounds that greet us.

Anger boils in my veins at the disastrous state of the stable. After a long day of treading on asphalt that's too rough for their hooves and carting people all around Cen-tral Park, oftentimes in weather that's way too hot, the horses return to dirty, cramped stalls. I grip the bars on the nearest stall and stare at poor overworked horses that can't defend themselves. The anger seeps out from my veins and pools in my belly as I spy empty troughs and mold growing on the walls. My magic crackles through my arm hair and hums behind my molars.

"This is a tragedy, Sinistro," I whisper, eyes never leaving the poor creatures. Tears collect in my lashes, and I swallow the lump in my throat. "We can't leave them like this."

"I take it you have a plan?" Sinistro hops up onto a ledge and peers down into the stall. "I wouldn't be surprised if you did."

"Well…not quite, but they aren't staying here. Madonna mia. This is animal abuse!"

"What's going on?" Moss asks from a few feet behind us.

"These poor horses," I say. "Look!"

Moss looks into the stables, sees the mistreated horses, and frowns. I can tell he sees what I see. "You're right. I agree a hundred percent," he says, but I can *also* tell he's hedging.

"But…?" I prompt.

Moss sighs. "I don't want to get into trouble, Giada. It's different for me than it is for you."

"What do you mean?"

"If the stable owner catches us, I'd be the one they'd blame. Not you or Jodi. It's why my mom's so afraid."

It takes me a moment to realize what Moss is saying and

another wave of anger washes over me. If we're caught, Moss would get in trouble before Jodi and me because of the color of his skin. Which is terrible and unfair.

I glance over at the horses and then back at him, saying, "I don't want anything to happen to you. We can just go to your school and figure out what to do next to follow the unicorn's trail."

Moss looks at the stables. I can see fury in his eyes—at the unjust mistreatment of helpless animals—that I know mirrors my own. After a moment he shakes his head. "Let's just be quick, okay?"

"Are you sure?" I ask. Even as my heart breaks at the thought of leaving these poor horses behind, I know I don't want to push Moss beyond his limits. And I also don't want him to feel obligated to do this.

"I'm sure," Moss says. "Let's do it."

With his okay, I let my magic loose. It burns in my core and shoots down my legs and up my arms. It pulses in my fingertips and sparks on my fingernails. I press my hands together and try to channel the wave of magic coursing through me.

Everything around me is drowned out by the rush of power building inside me. Goddess Diana is guiding my magic as it grows stronger. With her help, I take a deep breath and push my hands outward, feeling the magic surge against my palms like waves lashing at a boat. White light shoots from my hands and cuts through the padlocks securing each stall door. The stable fills with the smell of burning metal as the locks clank to the brick floor.

The stall doors fling themselves open and the horses stand still, unsure of what to do.

"You're free! You're all free!" I yell as I feel the magic deplete. A snack's definitely in order. Exhaustion replaces the feeling of power and I stifle a yawn with my arm before saying, "You don't have to pull tourists all over the park anymore."

Moss runs over to me and pats me on the shoulder. "That was freaking awesome," he says while pumping a fist in the air. "How'd you do that?"

I shrug, just as another yawn escapes from between my lips. "I was so angry about their living conditions, and I think Diana sensed it. I felt her strength mix with my magic. She helped me."

"What's going on?" Jodi pokes her head around the side of the stalls, taking in the broken locks and open doors. "I heard a lot of noise."

"We freed the horses," I say, wiping the sweat from my forehead with the back of my sleeve. "How's the investigation?"

"Oh, good call." She tilts her head to the side and says,

"I *think* I've got something, but I'm still checking it out. Be right back." With that, Jodi disappears before either of us can say anything to her.

"You really did it. I can't get over how rad that was," Moss says, turning to me. He paces around, the grin on his face huge. "This is the kind of stuff that gets me excited. Seeing how our magic can help all kinds of animals." He shakes his head, shoulders slumping a bit. Moss looks down at his palms and sighs. "It's just annoying that I can't always get mine to work."

"Your magic?" I ask carefully.

"Yeah." He squints up at the stable's ceiling. "I feel like all the frustration over trying to figure out the perfect treatment plan—" he takes a deep breath and closes his eyes "—and even the cramping and nausea, are like gunk in a drainpipe. Sometimes it can feel like my magic's backed up, unable to swirl through my body with ease. But some days, like today, I can still get it to work. The gunk's not gone, but maybe it's cleared up a little bit."

My heart squeezes. Seeing him so open is a nice change. "What makes today different than others?"

Moss pats the side of a white horse that's hanging out in a nearby stall and says, "I feel confident, being out in the real world, instead of practicing alone at home. I'm realizing that I don't always need to be home to be able to take care of myself. I can still do things my way. These past few weeks, I've really wanted to get back to how things used to be. But I think it's okay for things to change." He smiles and adds, "Yeah, there may be days where I feel terrible and can't get out of bed. But that's okay. My magic's not actually gone. I don't think it ever was."

"That's huge, Moss." A smile spreads across my face. "I'm proud of you."

He laughs, "You'll still have to put up with me being grumpy, though."

"I wouldn't have it any other way," I say with a roll of my eyes.

"Anyway…" Moss looks around the stable and scratches the back of his neck. His eyebrows quirk upward as he asks, "What do we do with them now?"

"The horses? I didn't think that through, really."

"So, you don't know what to do with…" Moss glances around the stalls as he quickly tallies the horses. His eyes widen. "Sixteen horses! Giada, we can't take care of sixteen horses on our own. And it's not like they can live in Central Park. Someone'll find them and bring them right back here."

"Someone should fine the owner of this business, is what should happen," I say while pulling out a wedge of parmesan and my water bottle from my backpack. I take a big bite of the cheese and close my eyes, enjoying the salty flavor as it hits my tongue. "It's atrocious!"

Moss looks around and hurries over to a shovel that he hastily jams through the entrance's door handles. "This'll buy us some time while we figure out what to do."

Fe flutters through the air before alighting near a dirty window. She whistles down to Moss. "Fe's got an idea," he says before he calls back to her. "What if we call the Jersey Devils to come pick up the horses and bring them somewhere safe? The Jersey Devils are much bigger than the horses. Stronger, too."

"Smart thinking," Sinistro says, swishing his tail. "Except how will we call them with your magic being near depleted? It's not like I can whistle."

I look at Moss, toying with my cornicello, and say, "I'm a little wiped out after the huge surge it took to free the horses. How are you feeling? Do you think you could call them again?"

"Me? On my own?" He shakes his head. "Let's not get ahead of ourselves. We were on their home turf when I did it earlier. They were nearby. I've never called a creature from this far before."

"You can do this, Moss," I say. "I know you can. Just take your time and nudge it along a bit further. Do you want to try?"

Moss only shrugs, his brow knit tight as he stares at the ground.

"You have Fe, too," I continue. "She's your familiar. That means her magic can make yours stronger and vice versa. Your bond's like a circle."

"I know. I'm feeling okay right now, and I'd like to give it another shot. It's just…" Moss toes at the dirt on the ground and shakes his head once more. "I've gotten so used to not being able to conjure it."

"You *have* magic. It hasn't gone away. You just said so yourself." I place a hand on his shoulder and smile. "It's just stuck. Like the drainpipe? You can unstick it."

"Okay. I'll try," Moss says, smiling. "We do need to help all these horses."

"Exactly!"

One by one, we coax the horses from their stalls and guide them out the back of the stable to an empty alley with two broken-down carriages and a nasty-smelling dumpster. I notice Jodi make her way back toward the empty stalls, but she doesn't follow us outside. Instead, she enters each stall to inspect them, though for what exactly I'm not sure.

Moss walks toward the alley's entrance and stops near a green bicycle leaned against the brick wall. Not many people walk past, and most are in a rush or too busy staring at their phones to notice us and the sixteen horses.

I follow Moss and slip my hand into his. Sinistro stands between us, his tail wrapped around Moss's leg, and Fe's on his shoulder. Moss grins and runs his other hand through his hair, saying, "I think I can do this. Can you use whatever energy you have left to help me along?"

"No, you *can* do this." I tighten my grip on his hand. "And yes, of course. Try closing your eyes and thinking about a pot of water on the stove. You've salted it and got it ready for the fettuccine, but now you just need it to boil. You're the stove, and your magic is the pot of water."

Moss laughs, but he closes his eyes. I do the same and picture my own stove back at home. I imagine our big metal pot on the front burner, with enough salt in the water to make the Dead Sea jealous. I focus on my magical core, on adjusting the fire under the pot and setting it to high. My magic's pretty much spent after using it to free the horses, but I can feel the little bit I've got left starting to bubble.

Moss's hand is clammy, and I can't sense his magic. Sinistro's and Fe's magic buzz against mine. It swirls between us, blending perfectly like basil and tomatoes. But Moss's isn't there. I plant my feet firmer on the asphalt and hold his hand until my own aches. Sweat pools under my arms as I try to focus everything on uncovering his magic. When I open one eye and look at Moss, he's sweating, too, and his mouth's pressed in a firm line, his jaw tense. A passing thought about Jodi and what she might have found wiggles its way into my mind. But I don't bring it up now. Behind us, the horses start to grow restless. A few snort while others kick at the dirty ground. I try not to pay them any attention and focus on bolstering Moss's magic, but anxiety blossoms in my stomach and I pray to Diana that no one notices the giant horses hidden in the alley's shadows. Fe twitters around Moss and he nods, slowly taking a breath in through his nose and releasing it from his mouth. He does this a few more times. His shoulders and jaw relax.

Just as I'm about to suggest we try something else I feel the smallest spark of Moss's magic ignite against my own. It flickers like a candle in a breeze, but gets stronger and soon mixes with mine, Sinistro's, and Fe's.

"It's working," I whisper, and I feel Moss squeeze my hand in response. "Are you ready to try the call?"

"Yeah, I think so." Moss laughs. "I haven't felt like this in a long time. Not even when I called them earlier. This feels different."

"We're working together side by side," I say. I open my eyes to see Moss looking at me, his grin wider than I've seen since I moved in with him and his parents.

"Yeah! It's awesome."

"Think of all the cool things we can do together! All the creatures we can rescue."

Without warning, Moss lets go of my hand and places his pinkies in his mouth. The call is crisp and clear and just as shrieky as it was back in Weehawken. I can feel our magic laced between the notes of his whistling. The call echoes off the alley's walls and bursts forth from the tiny space out into the sky. And then there's silence.

Moss furrows his brow and peeks around the alley's entrance. "Where are they? That definitely worked, right?"

"I think it did. It felt like it."

Neeeeiiiigh. Neeeeeiiiiigh.

"Shhh, horseys," I say. "It'll be okay."

"It's not the horses, Giada," Sinistro says, swishing through my legs.

I turn around to see the shiny black Jersey Devil, the one who communicated with us, perched on a fire escape that's groaning under his massive weight. "Moss!" I pat him on the shoulder, and he whips around, eyes wide as he spies the Jersey Devil.

"Holy cow," he mutters. "We did it!"

"*You* did it," I say.

We hurry over to the Jersey Devil as he shakes out his mane. His glances at the horses for a moment before his

145

gaze lands on us, head tilted slightly to the left as if questioning why we called.

My gaze bounces between Moss and the Jersey Devil. "Do you think you've got enough magic left to communicate with him?"

Moss looks down at his hands, flexing his fingers, and says, "I think I can do it, but I need a minute to grab some water and take a breather."

"Of course," I say as Moss pulls out his water bottle and rests against the stable's brick wall. I look at the fire escape and want the Jersey Devil to fly down into the alley, but maybe the horses make him nervous. I don't want to spook him. I bite my lip in thought and then realize what Moss will have to do. "Oh no, Moss. They don't want to come down. I think you're gonna have to climb the fire escape."

Moss's throat bobs as he looks at the distance between the fire escape's ladder and the ground. He puts his water bottle away and straightens. "It's pretty high up there."

"If you climb the dumpster, you can reach the ladder."

"This sounds like a terrible idea. Why don't you do it?" Moss crosses his arms over his chest and arches an eyebrow.

"Because my magic's not there yet. Yours is."

"What if I fall? Or what if the fire escape collapses under the Jersey Devil's weight?"

"I can heal you once my magic's recharged! I still have loads of guaritrice training under my belt."

Moss rolls his eyes. "We started out trying to save a unicorn and now we're saving a bunch of horses. This has become a whole thing."

"When duty calls, we must answer!" I shrug.

"Not helpful." Moss assesses the situation, hands on his hips, before walking over to the dumpster and inspecting its flimsy metal lid. He pulls over a couple apple crates and uses them as a way up on top of the dumpster. Carefully, Moss balances on his tiptoes and grasps the fire escape's ladder, pulling it down with a loud rumble.

"Good job!" I call just as Jodi wanders into the alleyway. Her eyebrows shoot up into her hairline as she takes in the scene.

"Uhh… I wasn't gone that long," she says, her gaze darting between the horses, Moss, and the Jersey Devil. "What's happening?"

"Where were you?" I ask, narrowing my eyes. "You were gone an awfully long time."

"I asked you first," Jodi counters. She stares at me for a long time before I finally relent.

"We didn't know what to do once we freed the horses,

so we called the Jersey Devils to help carry them some-where else." I walk over to a brown horse and rub its nose.

Jodi tilts her head to the side as if deep in thought be-fore nodding. "Smart. Jersey Devils are some of the stron-gest magical creatures local to the area."

"So did it end up being anything?" I ask, my eyes trained on Moss as he climbs the fire escape and carefully places a hand on the Jersey Devil's back.

"Yes, actually!" Jodi perks up, but before she can elabo-rate, Moss whistles down at us and waves an arm.

"Giada! Come here. I think I'll need your help commu-nicating with him."

I move closer to the dumpster and see Fe sitting on top of Moss's head. Sinistro's perched on top of the dump-ster, grooming his fluffy black fur. He trots over to me and nudges my hand with his head. "I can guide our magic up toward him with my tail. You won't have to climb all the way up."

I hold on to Sinistro's back and conjure my magic once more. It's still not fully recharged, but there's enough to help bolster Moss's. It blends with Sinistro's and I can feel it pulse between us like twin heartbeats. I feel Moss's and Fe's magic, too, as it vibrates outward. Sinistro's tail twitches, his fur standing on end like he was just electro-cuted, as he points it toward Moss and Fe. Moss's magic pulses stronger than it did when he made the call, almost as if exercising it has made it more powerful. Our help might not be as strong as if we were holding on to Moss, but it should be enough.

Moss puts a hand on the Jersey Devil's side and closes his eyes, taking the time to breathe slowly, as if meditating. After a moment, the Jersey Devil's magic pushes back against ours. It's heavy, but clear. Like a stone sinking in a lake. He's communicating with Moss.

"They'll help us," Moss calls down from the fire escape. "The other Jersey Devils are nearby—they stayed close to the city in case we needed help."

"Amazing! Are they gonna fly down?"

"They can, but they won't land on the ground. They're afraid of the New York creatures."

"But they can help?" I confirm.

Moss nods and gives the Jersey Devil a firm pat before carefully climbing down the fire escape and hopping gently onto the dumpster. He jumps down in front of Sinistro and me, a grin on his face. "I did it! Again!"

"How do you feel?" I ask, my question filled with concern as I take in his pale complexion and sweaty brow. "Are you okay?"

"I'm queasy. Ugh. We're going to need to find another bathroom soon." He grabs his water bottle again and takes a huge gulp. "But still, I feel strong. It's a strange combo for sure."

I high-five Moss before pulling a bag of hard-boiled eggs out of my backpack, taking one for myself before handing it to him. "Do you want to eat something?" I say through a mouthful of egg. I packed these in my bag last minute when I saw a few extra sitting in the fridge. They're one of Moss's go-to snacks, and I love them, too.

Moss takes out one of the eggs and bites into it with relish just as the Jersey Devil leaps off the fire escape and high into the sky. *Neeeeiiiigh. Neeeeiiiigh.* His call echoes around us and the horses' ears perk, a few of them looking up at the giant flying beast. Soon, the sky darkens with several more of the creatures as they hover over the alley.

I wave an arm up at them and watch as one by one the Jersey Devils snatch the horses up in their grasp like a claw machine at a diner and carry them into the air. Surprisingly, the horses don't make much of a fuss. They trust the Jersey Devils to protect them.

"I told him to bring the horses to the Pine Barrens. It's quiet and there are plenty of farms and open space."

"They'll like that." I grin as the last horse gets picked up and flown off after its friends. "You did a great job."

Moss smiles, his face flushing before taking another bite of his egg.

Jodi clears her throat and says, "I hate to interrupt." She adjusts her witch's hat and smirks. "But I've found something you both have to see."

My stomach twists and I can't believe I got us so far off track from finding the unicorn. We need to hustle. "What is it?"

"Poop," Jodi exclaims before pulling out a bag of red grapes to snack on.

"Poop?" Moss and I say in unison.

Rather than elaborating, she turns on her heel and walks back into the stable—Moss, Fe, Sinistro, and I hurrying after her.

10

Jodi wasn't joking. In the very last stall on the left, amid dirty old hay and scattered horse feed, is a small pile of poop. I've only ever seen unicorn feces in a book my nonna gave me called *Their Business Is Our Business: A Magical Zoologist's Guide to Creatures' Bodily Functions* by Caitlin Bonner. The book goes into detail about the properties and uses we have for magical creatures' waste, and how different creatures' feces might affect the growth patterns and strength of certain plants. There are even diagrams! And it's not just a book for gardening—though that's what my nonna used it for. For example, the author describes how dragon feces, if properly dried and processed, can be used in alchemy spells to create gold.

The point is, unicorn feces—like everything attributed to unicorns—is rare. Though less rare than other things like their hair and horns. The way you can tell a unicorn's poop from other creatures' is how it shines. It looks completely ordinary until sunlight hits it and then the feces glitter like silver. In the moonlight, they shine even brighter. That's why, if you're in need of unicorn feces, it's best to search for it at night. It's also a good idea to bring an albino ferret with you. Like truffle pigs, albino ferrets can be trained to sniff out unicorn feces. It's a remarkable skill of theirs that no one ever talks about.

And why might a person need unicorn feces? Well, it's quite versatile for spells and potions. Oracles can use it when going into trances, sharpening their visions of future events. Streghe who follow Venus might dust it on their arms and necks to charm lovers during Lupercalia. Even fixers use it. For me, unicorn feces is especially helpful for attracting other extraordinary creatures in an area. Guaritori rub it on their palms before casting Morte al Incubo, a spell that obliterates a patient's nightmares and brings them a lifetime of restful sleep.

And here it is, right in front of me. This pile of what appears to be horse poop that most people wouldn't cast a second glance. But, upon closer inspection, it's obvious that it belongs to a unicorn. There's a slight silver shimmer as a ray of sunlight falls over it. The poop sparkles unlike any jewelry I've ever seen. It's actually very pretty.

"The unicorn was here!" I say excitedly, kneeling in front of it to get a better look. "It looks fresh, but not *too* fresh."

"How can you tell?" Jodi asks.

"Well, unicorn poop is like cat poop." Sinistro shoots me a look, but I continue, saying, "It gets all dry and hard after a few hours. Plus, look at how it shines in the sunlight. It's all silvery."

"You don't have to announce it to the whole world," Sinistro whines, ducking his head from embarrassment.

"Sorry," I whisper to him.

"Oh, that's gross," Jodi says.

Moss and I both shrug.

I pull a plastic sandwich bag out of my backpack. With care, I pick up the unicorn feces with the bag and zip it shut before putting it away. Jodi raises her eyebrows and I shrug again. "It has a lot of uses! We can't just not take it."

Moss clears his throat and says, "So she was moved recently?"

"Within the last one to three hours." I pull out some hand sanitizer and rub it on my palms.

"Where could she have gone?" Moss kicks at the hay and curses under his breath. He looks at Jodi. "Let me see the business card from your Madre?" She pulls the card out from her pocket and hands it over to him. Moss flips it around in his hand, inspecting it closely. "What if we set him up? Like people do in movies?"

"What do you mean?" I ask.

"We could get ahold of this Joe guy—he left the card for Madre to call him, after all. Like, we could offer him something he might want. Maybe say we're interested in helping him with the medicine he's developing."

"And we can insist on seeing the unicorn, too." I jump to my feet, invigorated by Moss's plan. "This is a great idea."

Jodi takes the card back from Moss and squints at it. "But how do we even get ahold of Joe? There's no phone number or address."

"The seventeen on the card has to mean *something*," Moss says. "Otherwise, the Madre del Malocchio wouldn't have been able to contact him again either."

"All I know is seventeen is a *very* unlucky number in Italy. Like how you Americans are superstitious over the number thirteen."

"He didn't say what it meant when he talked to Madre." Jodi shakes her head, worrying her bottom lip with her teeth. Suddenly, her green eyes widen, and she jumps up on the balls of her feet. "But! Madre has said in the past there are various ways to communicate with others magically. The Streghe del Malocchio never use phones, and letters can take forever getting from city to city through our underground passageways. She's said there are faster methods."

"What if that's what the business card is for? A different method?" I ask.

Jodi nods with enthusiasm. "I think that must be it. But I don't know what it could be. Madre never explained further."

"Let's research it when we get to my old school," Moss suggests. "The library has tons of books about everything and anything you could need."

"Yes!" I pump my fist in the air. "Let's do it." My heart hammers hard against my rib cage as the excitement works its way through my body. We're finally getting somewhere. And soon the unicorn will be back safely with us.

After a bathroom break and a snack at a nearby deli, we make our way toward Bryant Park where the New York Public Library stands. The library is an old gray building that looks almost out of place alongside the tall skyscrapers jutting up like sunflowers all around it. But it's probably my favorite building in all of New York City. Moss and his parents took me to the library on my first visit into the city, but we didn't go into Moss's old school. They only said it was around here. I was too distracted walking down the rows and rows of books to fully register that they even said anything about his school.

All libraries have a magic of their own. There's something special about that musty smell that lingers on your clothes hours after you leave, the calming quiet and hushed conversations that sound like spellcasting, and the millions of books that serve as portals to any world you can imagine. If I could live anywhere, it would be in the aisles of a well-stocked library.

But Moss doesn't lead us up to the library's entrance. Instead, he stops just in front of the left lion statue that stands at the bottom of the stone stairs. The lion is fearsome, even if he's made from stone, with a thick long mane and hulking body. He holds his head up with pride, staring down at everyone from his position lying on his pedestal. Sinistro hops up next to the statue and mirrors the lion's regal pose.

"How do I look?" he asks, lifting his chin just a bit higher. "Do I look like the king of the jungle?"

I giggle and rub Sinistro's head.

"Is your school inside?" Jodi asks.

Moss shakes his head. "Kind of—the school's underneath the library. This is the entrance."

I look around the lion statue and his pedestal, tilting my head. "Where's the door?"

"This is my favorite part," Moss says with a grin. "The lions protect the two entrances inside. You have to present yourself to the lion with a bow. He'll make sure you're a magical being. Then!" His dark eyes glint with excitement and I can't help but get excited, too. "Then he'll ask you a riddle to get into the school."

"Riddles?" Jodi looks between us and sighs. "I'm no good at those."

"We can enter as a group. I happen to be great at riddles. I read all the Batman comics with the Riddler in them for practice before starting my first day of school when I was seven years old. I was so nervous," he laughs. "But the lions are good-natured about it, too. They adjust the riddles' difficulty based on the age of who they're asking. One time, when I was eight, I spent twenty minutes out here trying to solve the riddle. An older kid had to help me."

"This is fun!" I say, taking a step closer to the lion. I look over my shoulder at the busy sidewalk and street. Surely someone will see us talking to the lion. "How do we do this without people noticing?"

Moss shrugs. "No one ever does. The lions ward against the curiosity of non-magical folk. People simply turn away or will see past us and up to the library."

"Fascinating!" I bow at the lion's feet before pressing a hand to his mane, the stone warming underneath it. A low growl vibrates against my palm as the lion clears his throat, twisting his head to look down at us with an air of majesty.

"Good afternoon, children." His voice is deep and rumbles like thunder. The lion's eyes land on Fe and Sinistro and he pauses, before adding, "And animals. To what do I owe the pleasure?"

"We're here to enter the school," I say. My magic thrums between my ribs like violin strings and I can already feel it pulsing alongside the stone lion's.

"The Irving School of Magic," Moss adds.

"The one and only." The lion paws at his pedestal, his ears twitching. "Very well. Gather round and let me first ensure you're truly magical."

Moss, Jodi, and Fe move closer to Sinistro and me. Jodi and Moss put their hands on the stone lion, Fe adds a wing, and the lion hums for a moment before deliberating. "Hmm. Good, good. You all passed the first test. Now onto the real challenge."

The lion clears his throat, eyes sweeping over us indulgently. Clearly this is the part the lion relishes most. "What is it that, given one, you'll have either two or none?"

Moss scratches his chin, eyes narrow in thought. On the road, a cabbie honks her horn as another car cuts her off. People hurry past us, their eyes either focused straight ahead, on their phones, or distractedly staring up at the library. No one even glances at us.

Finally, Moss snaps his fingers and assurance alights on his face. "I got it! It's a choice."

The lion nods. "Very good."

Cracks form in the lion's pedestal, and a white light seeps through. The cracks take the shape of a door about four feet tall. Moss places a gentle hand on the stone and presses. The door swings open and he gestures for Jodi, Sinistro, and me to head inside first. We bend down and take a few cramped steps with our heads ducked and shoulders hunched before the small entryway opens into a beautiful foyer.

The foyer is gigantic—it's three stories high. Warm sunlight pools in from floor-to-ceiling windows that make no sense considering Moss said we're underneath the New York Public Library. Especially since the Streghe del Malocchio live in darkness all the way underground. But it must be some kind of enchantment that a building fixer put on the windows.

The floors are black-and-white-checkered marble like a chessboard. Two grand mahogany staircases curve down a few feet in front of us. Curio cabinets stuffed with oddities line every wall and on the second floor are a collection of doors that must lead to classrooms or offices. Above our heads, dipping between the two staircases, is a large crystal chandelier that twinkles in the light. And flying above the chandelier are enchanted books of various shapes and sizes, zooming through the air like birds.

Velvet couches and armchairs are tucked into corners, some occupied by students in deep discussions. More students pass through the foyer—books and papers in hand as they go about their days. Some of them are as young as seven years old, but surprisingly there are quite a few older than thirteen, which is odd since everyone graduates from my school and takes the oath at that age. Then it dawns on me that there's another big difference between this school and my own—Moss has never said his school was *only* for guaritori. And that makes sense considering he's a magical veterinarian and began his training once Fe found him and he realized his calling.

"Wow," I breathe, doing a twirl to take in the entire room. I don't even want to blink for fear of missing something. "This is extraordinary."

"I've never been somewhere like this," Jodi exclaims. "It's so different from Olde Yorque."

Moss emerges from the short entrance into the foyer and laughs upon seeing the shock on our faces. "Welcome to the Irving School of Magic!"

11

Moss leads us down a winding corridor, its walls stuffed with portraits of different kinds of streghe showcasing their skills. One strega stands in front of a black scrying mirror, tarot cards in between her long fingers. Another strega poses from atop a flying ship with a great big balloon and sparkling nets hanging from its side. And there's another strega in a room with several different kinds of instruments, some I don't even recognize. He's grinning, one hand atop a piano and another holding what looks like a magical lute of some kind.

"Your school isn't just for magical healers?" I ask, tearing my eyes away from the portraits and glancing at Moss.

"It's for all magical folk. You start here when you're five and take general classes until you begin showing an inclination toward a specialty. I learned a lot about different things like astrology, fortune-telling, and magical botany. At first, I specialized in healing because it's what my dad does, and I liked it. But then Fe came along a year after I started taking healing classes—" Moss grins and strokes a finger down the bird's neck "—and I switched my specialty to magical veterinarian courses. You graduate from that track at thirteen, too. But some witches stay in school until at least twenty years old here. And then some come back later in life to specialize in other magics."

My head swims with all the possibilities and the freedom to choose your own path. Envy jabs at my side—I wish I had gone to a school like this. One where we could learn whatever we wished and focus on where our talents led us. My school was only for guaritori. You went from ages seven to thirteen and learned all about healing humans. Nothing else. For me, the lessons were long, boring, and frustrating. Alessia loved them, but I hated it. When your six years were up, you'd take your oath and immediately start your apprenticeship. For us students, there could be no discussion about other specialties or what we may want to do with our magic. (Until I came along, that is.)

"In Italy, streghe usually follow tradition and honor the same god or goddess their family has forever."

Moss shrugs. "It's different here. We have a little more say in the matter, but predisposition for a specific kind of magic is common. Sometimes, people have talents for more than one magic. Like how I'm also skilled in the kind of magical singing my mom does."

"But what about the gods?" I ask, eager to learn more about American witches. "Don't they feel slighted if you're not loyal to only one?"

"We don't place as much emphasis on those traditions here. The guaritori do maybe more than others, but most focus on honing the magic in their bodies and the energy that comes from the earth, stars, sun, and moon."

"But what about the extra strength a god or goddess provides? Diana has blessed me with power in times that I've needed help."

"The gods also punish if they feel any kind of disrespect whereas if you depend on your own magic or the natural world's, you'll never run into that problem."

I remember how Diana disciplined me after misusing her magic in Malafi when defending Sinistro and me against a Strega del Malocchio in the marketplace. But she also protected Alessia and me when moon beckoning. It's an ever-evolving negotiation, tying your magic to a particular god or goddess. You give and you take. Sometimes it's to your benefit, other times it's to theirs. I can see why American witches might not feel the urge to take an oath and bind their magic in that way.

Moss takes a left into what can only be described as the grandest library I've ever seen. Bookshelves are built into each wall—there are no windows in this room. Bookshelves even cover the ceiling, the books safe from falling thanks to magic and accessible by floating platforms that carry a person up from the floor. Books flutter overhead, some leaping from their shelves and zipping out of the room and down the corridor. Others flap their pages around the library and alight on desks or drop into the hands of students. As we move in farther, I get a whiff of old paper and dust—smells that conjure up memories of every library I've ever been to. Chairs, couches, and tables are tucked away into corners or hidden by bookcases that make the library feel like a labyrinth. Candelabras provide some light, but most of it comes from the brass chandelier that hangs from the one space on the ceiling where there are no books. But there are still places that I can't see, places where shadows fall on the shelves concealing magical books. My heart thrums with excitement as I crane my neck around the room to take in everything.

"Your school's so cool," Jodi whispers. "I wish I went here."

"Me, too," I say. "This might be even more impressive than the library above us."

"It's alright, I guess." Moss grins, putting his hands in his pockets.

"Only alright?" I raise a brow.

"Okay, it's maybe my favorite place ever. I miss going to school," he says. "I just love learning. Maybe someday, after I've finished my apprenticeship and worked as a magical vet for a few years, I'll come back and specialize in something else."

I smile at Moss. I feel lucky, getting to see him in his element like this.

Moss looks at his phone and frowns. "It's getting late." He shows his phone screen to Jodi and me. The time— and several missed calls and texts from his parents—shine bright in the dim library.

"Ugh. How's it almost nine already?" I close my eyes, anxiety creeping under my skin. Madonna mia. Alessia's been in Olde Yorque for hours now and I have no way to get ahold of her because phones don't work down there.

Ever since freeing the horses, it's felt like my magic's been flitting around my belly like butterflies and I haven't quite been able to bounce back like I normally do. I've tried to ignore it, but part of me wonders if it's because of my bargain with Angie. What if Alessia's having trouble

166

getting Angie's purse? We're getting closer to the deadline. What if this strange feeling is my magic slowly trickling away?

Sinistro rubs up against my legs and I'm unsure if he can sense my magic's weirdness. "Do you think we're going back home tonight?"

I bend down to scritch his ears and shake my head. "I don't think so." I stand up, looking at Moss and Jodi, and say, "I think we're going to have to spend the night researching."

Moss rubs at his temples, his jaw tense and shoulders rigid. "What about my parents? They're gonna be so mad. They probably already are. I'm surprised they haven't tracked my location and dragged us back home yet."

Jodi turns around in a circle, stopping when her eyes land on the circulation desk. A large smile that reminds me of Malafi's Madre curls over her lips. "Would they be less angry if you had the librarian call them?"

"Actually, that's not a bad idea," Moss says, brightening. "Mrs. Bhandari's like my mom's best friend. They'd feel a lot better knowing we're here and safe with her. Probably buy us some time, too."

"Can I go explore before we settle in?" Jodi asks.

Moss nods. "Go for it but come find us soon. We'll call my mom and then get to business. We need to figure out how to contact this guy."

Jodi disappears down an aisle while we walk over to the circulation desk.

Mrs. Bhandari's wavy black hair is tied in a low pony-tail that hangs down her back. She wears a cream-colored cardigan and cerulean blouse that complement her cool brown skin. She's busy looking through a large and dusty book when we approach, her thick eyebrows furrowed in thought. But she greets Moss when he catches her eye. "Moss! What're you doing here so late?" She looks at me with large brown eyes, giving me a warm smile. "Is this Giada?"

"Buona sera," I say. "How'd you know me?"

"Jasmine, Moss's mom, has told me all about you!"

"You're working awfully late," Moss says, clearly avoiding what he needs to ask her.

She shrugs. "Night shift. You know how the library is. Always open, always busy."

I nudge Moss's arm and he stumbles forward a bit. "Well, speaking of my mom…" Moss scratches the back of his neck, not quite looking Mrs. Bhandari in the eye. "Could you possibly call her and let her know we're safe with you in the library? And that we need to stay overnight since we got caught up in studying?" he blurts out in a rush.

"Massimo Calamoneri." The smile drops from Mrs. Bhandari's face, and she narrows her gaze. "Are you telling me your parents don't know you're here?"

"Well, I did text her a few hours ago and told her we were here," Moss says, blushing.

"A few *hours* ago?" Mrs. Bhandari repeats.

"It was my idea," I explain and she looks at me, a doubtful eyebrow raised. "I wanted to see this incredible library and do some research on rarer animal healing practices." I flash my most charming smile and add, "It really is the most beautiful library I've ever seen. Better, even, than the one at my old school."

Mrs. Bhandari's expression softens and she turns back to Moss. "I know what it was like growing up here. It's tempting to want to explore with your friends. Your mom and I did it all the time. Did Moss tell you I attended Irving with his mom?" She laughs, shaking her head. "That was a long time ago, though."

"So will you call her?" Moss asks.

"Fine, but you'll stay here until morning. No running through the city in the middle of the night. It's too dangerous. There are some spare dorm rooms for you to sleep in. Because you *will* be resting."

Moss pumps a fist in the air, a huge smile on his face. "Thank you, thank you, thank you!"

"I'm not promising she won't be upset," Mrs. Bhandari warns. "But I'll try to smooth things over best I can."

"You're the best, Mrs. Bhandari."

"I know I am."

Mrs. Bhandari pulls out her phone and she waves for us to head along. With that settled, Moss looks a lot more at ease as he leads me past a bunch of tables where students are busy working.

"I wonder what Jodi's up to?" I ask. "Do you think her parents want to know where *she's* at? Maybe sneaking around's normal for her."

"You need to ease up on her," Moss whispers. "She's nice. A little flaky, maybe, but not distrustful like you think."

I shrug. "You don't know the Streghe del Malocchio like I do."

"But Jodi's been nothing but helpful to us. You're judging her unfairly, based on things other witches did to you. That wasn't her, Giada," Moss says. "I know what that's like and it's awful. Stereotypes aren't cool."

Guilt rolls around in my stomach. "Ugh. You're right. What happened last year wasn't her fault, after all."

"I'm always right," Moss says with a laugh. "Just chill out a bit and you'll see that she's been great."

We walk along in silence. Sinistro flicks his tail against my legs and prances ahead of us. He whips his head back to glance at me and says, "Do you see the other familiars, Giada? How exciting!"

I look at the table he's staring at and sure enough there

are three animals hanging out alongside their humans. A goldendoodle puppy, a chameleon, and a Flemish giant rabbit sit around the table occasionally nudging their humans in conversation or for pets. I stop in my tracks, my heart beating faster as a large smile spreads across my face. I've never seen so many streghe like me. It was lonely, hiding my dreams of becoming a magical vet from my family. Alessia knew, but even then, I kept things from her.

Sadness twinges in my stomach and I remember Maestra Vita and my other instructors. They didn't understand me. If I'd gone to a place like the Irving School of Magic, I could've learned so much more about my magic and myself so much sooner. Maybe Moss is onto something. Maybe one day, after I complete my apprenticeship and open my own clinic, I can come back here and take some classes.

"Giada?" Moss whispers and I snap out of my thoughts.

"Sorry," I say with a laugh, hurrying to catch up to Moss and Fe. "This place is fabulous, and I never want to leave."

"Do you want to see the coolest thing in here?" Moss asks while guiding us to the room's center where a large map of the library sits atop a pedestal. It glows a soft blue and is detailed enough to show every single book on every single shelf in the entire library. The map even shows the books that flit around the ceiling and sit open on tables or desks. To the left of the map is a list of hundreds of titles. I run my fingers down the list and they shimmer silver as I touch them.

"Is this how you find books?"

"Yeah, exactly. When you're not sure what you're looking for, you can tap in a few keywords and the books that are most relevant will fly off the shelves over to you. And if there's a relevant section, that'll light up on the map. If someone else has one of the books you need, it'll show up on the map, but won't fly over. And the list of books on the left are ones that are currently checked out of the library."

"Madonna mia. This is so clever. At my school, we just looked up books the old-fashioned way."

"This map saved me in school. It was so much easier than searching through rows and rows of books." Moss shrugs. "But some people here still do that. I think they just like being in the library. Can't blame them for that."

Moss taps in a few words like *magical communication*, *magical business cards*, and *numerology*. In an instant, books start to fly off their shelves and flap above us in a circle. The books begin to dip lower and one of them politely nudges me with its spine. I open my arms to it and the book lands gently. Several other books touch down on top of the first one, stacking themselves neatly in my hands. Moss has his own stack of at least a dozen books, too. "Look," Moss says, nodding to the map. "There's a whole section on magical communication. Let's find a table near there and get started."

He guides us toward the back right of the library, toward a dimly lit corner. Tucked away is a small table the four of us crowd around. Sinistro hops into a chair and Fe alights on Sinistro's head, the pair muttering to one another as Moss and I arrange the books on the table. Moss throws the business card on the table, its gold rim glinting in the faint light. He takes a seat, but I can't stop myself from pacing—the urgency bouncing around my body is too much. We've got paragraphs and paragraphs of information to read.

The minutes tick by as we search through book after book. We read up on communicating through astral projection and find a chart detailing the power of each number in existence. Moss takes advantage of our proximity to a clean, familiar bathroom with regular trips when he needs them, and I'm glad we finally got him to a place where he feels comfortable and safe. We go down a rabbit hole on how the pulp in paper can be infused with magic through things like vampire blood, banshee breath, or even shedded basilisk skin. We even learned that the pulp itself could be replaced with pixie and star dusts or crushed leviathan scales. At some point, Jodi finds us and plops down in the seat next to Sinistro and Fe.

"Did you call your mom, too?" I ask her as I munch on some cocoa-dusted almonds. "To let her know you'd be spending the night at Irving?"

Jodi shakes her head as she pulls out a granola bar and her water bottle. "I texted her that I was getting dinner with my cousin and then spending the night at my aunt's in Olde Yorque."

"She was cool with that?" Moss's eyes widened. He's picking at a bag of rice cakes.

"The Streghe del Malocchio keep weird hours." She shrugs. "My mom's used to it by now." Jodi says nothing else, pulling a notebook and pen from her bag. She grabs one of the books from our pile and begins taking notes on her reading.

After a couple hours, my back starts to hurt, and my fingers have gone raw from turning so many pages. I squeeze my eyes shut and open them again, blinking rapidly. Fatigue expands through my legs and arms, making them feel like jelly, and all the books I've read through haven't given us any clues on what this Joe guy's business card could mean or how we can get in touch with him.

"Need a break?" Moss asks while stretching his arms over his head. "I'm gonna hit the bathroom real quick, but then get back to it. I can study like this for hours. Go take a walk around the library."

I roll my eyes at him. "Of course you can. You're a nerd."

"Nerds are cool." Moss shrugs, pulling a pair of earbuds out of his backpack and switching to the music app on his phone before heading off in the direction of the restrooms.

"I'll come with you," Jodi offers. I smile at her as she leaves her notes and book open to the page she was reading. Sinistro yawns and kicks out his back legs before jumping down from his chair to join us. Together, we begin our walk around the library, starting on the perimeter and making our way back to the center before checking the library map and heading up the stairs to the Magical Creatures section.

"Let's look for some books on unicorns," I say while skimming over various titles—some of which I have back at home in my bedroom. I pull a couple books that look helpful and add, "There's a high likelihood that the unicorn will be injured, and we'll need to heal her." I ignore the concerned voice in the back of my head whispering about the possibility of the unicorn being dead. Anger bubbles up in my stomach and I take a deep breath to tamp it down. We don't know yet if she has any serious injuries or if she was killed by this horrible man and his organization. All we can do now is prepare for any possible outcome.

Jodi frowns, tugging at one of her blond curls. "I'd hate to see anything bad happen to a unicorn. They seem like such sweet, gentle creatures."

"They're very gentle. Though they're also known to stab predators with their horns when threatened," I say. "There was a group of poachers in northern France back in the late 1800s that tracked a blessing of unicorns through the Forest of Haguenau. The poachers' bodies were found, and it wasn't pretty." A shudder runs through my body remembering the diagrams in one of my unicorn books. "Non-magical folk thought it was bears, but there were signs—like hair and the state of the poachers' wounds— that made it clear to those in the know that it was unicorns."

"Oof. That's kind of cool, though. Knowing unicorns can defend themselves." Jodi shrugs her shoulders as she runs her fingers across a row of books. "Maybe this unicorn was able to defend herself, too."

A surprised laugh escapes from my throat and I shake my head even though I agree with her. "No wonder you're training to be a Strega del Malocchio. You're fiercer than you let on."

Jodi turns to me and gives a small curtsy. "The Streghe

del Malocchio aren't all doom and gloom, you know. We have layers like everyone else."

"They kidnapped my brother, best friend, and family," I say, looking at the ground.

"They shouldn't have done that," she begins, grabbing a book on cryptids found in the American South and idly turning through its pages. "But we're not all the same."

I pull the book *Unicorns and You: The Extraordinary Bond between Human and Creature,* by Dr. Melinda Newman, from the shelf and add it to my stack.

"I know and I realize I'm being unfair," I say. "After what I went through last year, it's just harder for me to trust."

Jodi frowns and fiddles with a heart-shaped pendant around her neck. She looks sad, as if she's been on the receiving end of this kind of wariness before, and my heart squeezes at the thought. It's not about her, really, and I don't want to upset her.

"I wish you weren't," she says. "We're no different from any other kind of witches. We just have stricter rules because of the scales. But we aren't this one single force that thinks the same and does the same things. We're all unique. And I want to help you." She scrunches her nose. "I kind of think the Madre does, too, in her own way."

"What do you mean?" I ask, my brow furrowing.

"I overheard her discussion with her inner circle of

streghe after that man left. She was furious about what he asked of her," Jodi explains. "She doesn't want to hurt any animals. But she couldn't do anything to stop him either, because of the scales." She tilts her head, adding, "You were right, in a way—I just think it's awfully coincidental that she left that business card out in such an obvious place right when she asked me to follow you, is all."

I stop walking as her explanation sinks in. Maybe the Madre couldn't be the one to help us, but she could send her Strega del Malocchio *in training* instead, if indirectly. Someone whose involvement wouldn't upend the scales. Interesting. It *would* be just like the Madre to do something so sneaky…

"Did you want to be a Strega del Malocchio?" I ask, hurrying to catch up with Jodi. "Like, doesn't living underground and giving up your name make you uncomfortable?"

"It's all I've ever known. My aunt and cousin are Streghe del Malocchio. They were the ones who recognized my potential to become one when I was little. I feel at home underground. Like it's where I'm meant to be. It's peaceful in Olde Yorque," Jodi says. "Besides, I love the sisterhood. We're the only coven that are all women. The Streghe del Malocchio may be scary to outsiders, but we have each other's backs. Unless there's a betrayal, of course. But I don't plan on doing anything like that." She scrunches her nose. "Plus my magic aligns with theirs—it just feels right. Like the first breath after being underwater or going to sleep in your own bed after months away from home. It's not a glamorous job. No one really likes us. But someone's got to take responsibility for the scales."

I pause my search for unicorn books and stare at Jodi as she continues searching the bookshelves. Even though I may not always agree with the Streghe del Malocchio and their methods of achieving balance, I can't knock Jodi's excitement. It reminds me of how I talk about being a magical vet—it might not be what others wanted for me at first, but it just makes sense. I grin at her before I can stop myself, and say, "That's kind of cool. You seem passionate about it."

"I am. I think there's a lot I can do as a Strega del Malocchio. I want to use my powers to maintain stability."

Jodi beams at me, seeming to put the whole matter to bed, before returning to her perusal of the bookshelves. Her eyebrow furrows as she picks up a familiar-looking book with a glossy red cover and faded silver title that reads *Spells and Potions for Untamed Beasts*. It's a book my nonna got me when I was little, one of my first books on healing creatures. She was a guaritrice but was also more interested in her garden and the magical creatures who lived in it.

"That's a good one. Let's add it to our pile." I look through a few of the books' glossaries and frown. "I haven't read all these books, but just from skimming it doesn't seem like a lot is known about healing unicorns. I guess that makes sense."

"Will that be a problem?" Jodi asks.

"Hopefully it isn't much different from healing a regular horse or quadrupedal mammal."

"Do we have the right supplies?"

I chew on my bottom lip, trying to remember what I have in my backpack. "I brought some stuff. I always do. And it should be what we need, though whether I have enough is a different story."

"Maybe she won't be injured. Maybe this man didn't hurt her."

"Maybe he's just waiting for the right time to do it." I grimace and my stomach flips over. The thought of this man killing vulnerable creatures to create medicine makes me nauseous.

Sinistro rubs up against my legs and I lean down to scritch between his ears. If someone ever took him, well, I don't know what I'd do. It would be like losing part of my soul. Just the idea makes me want to cry.

"There you are!" Moss's voice echoes down the aisle. I turn around in time to see him walking toward us, book in hand and Fe on his shoulder. He takes out an earbud and pauses his music before saying, "It's midnight." Moss yawns and rubs the back of his neck. "I'm super tired. It'll be good for us to rest up."

"Already?" I ask, surprised. "It's impossible to know what time it is in here."

We make our way back to our table where Mrs. Bhandari's standing, hands on her hips. "Off to bed, you three." She looks at Moss and winks. "All is well. But your mom is adamant about you getting a good night's sleep."

I stare at the books and notes laid out in front of us and then back at Moss. Part of me is tempted to push through the night and find a solution, but I know we should go to bed after all we did today.

Moss tucks the book in his backpack and nods for Jodi, Sinistro, and me to follow him and Mrs. Bhandari.

We walk out of the library and through twisting, turning hallways until we reach a sprawling marble staircase that leads to more twisting, turning hallways. Finally, after what feels like hours, Mrs. Bhandari stops in front of a row of three doors with glimmering, gold numbers hanging on them. With a flourish of her hand, the numbers transform into our names—*Moss*, *Giada*, and *Jodi*.

"The beds are pretty comfortable and there's a bathroom with necessities at the very end of the hall," Mrs. Bhandari explains. "Breakfast starts at 7 a.m.—Moss knows where the dining hall is. Sleep well and I'll be sure to check on you before I leave."

With that, she leaves the three of us outside our assigned dorm rooms. Sinistro paws at the door with my name on it and I open it a bit for him to wiggle inside. "We gotta figure this out tomorrow," I say, pressing my fingers to my temples. "The unicorn, Alessia, my magic… everything depends on us." Nerves swirl in my belly and I take a deep breath. It's going to be hard sleeping tonight.

Moss places a hand on my shoulder. "We can do this, okay?"

"Yeah, we won't fail," Jodi adds. "Promise."

I nod before slipping inside my room. I flick on the light, and close the door, my back pressed against it as I sink to the ground. Sinistro comes over and nudges his way into my lap, his purring loud and comforting as it vibrates against my skin. Fear and exhaustion tug at my eyes and I snuggle into Sinistro, my fingers tracing the cornicello hanging from my neck.

"I hope they're right," I whisper into the quiet room.

12

The dining hall is a huge room with stained glass windows glittering a rainbow of colors from the early afternoon sun—another enchantment that must come from a building fixer like in Irving's foyer. I try not to get too anxious about how late we all slept in—so late that we missed breakfast! Luckily, breakfast-for-lunch is popular at Moss's school. After loading my plate with eggs, bacon, and fruit in the food line and getting some tuna for Sinistro, I walk over to a well-worn wooden table where Jodi and Moss are already sitting. Jodi's cutting up a golden-brown waffle coated in a healthy layer of maple syrup and Moss is midbite on a piece of toast covered in smashed avocado and scrambled eggs. Both have books open on the table, reading while they eat.

I pour a cup of coffee—and pull out my own book. A thin tome with brittle pages about the meaning of the number seventeen written by a monk in the fifteenth century. After a few minutes, Mrs. Bhandari approaches. She has her purse slung over her arm and stifles a yawn with the back of her hand. "My shift's long over, but I wanted to wait to see you all before heading out." She looks at Moss's plate and nods. "Oh, good. Your mom texted a little bit ago to make sure you ate. She's glad you all got some rest. Are those foods okay?"

"Yeah," Moss says with a shrug. "Eggs, white toast, and avocado don't bother me much."

"Great! Well, it was nice meeting you, Giada and Jodi. Your parents are expecting you home by dinner. Don't make me into a liar!" Mrs. Bhandari levels us with a meaningful look before heading back out the large copper dining hall doors.

We glance at each other nervously—will we be able to get home in time?—finish our very late breakfast and, after filling up our water bottles, stocking up on snacks, and using the bathroom, we head back to the library for more in-depth research.

"Don't worry too much about my parents," Moss says

before we settle in. "At least not until we get home. We've got a ton to get done. They love Mrs. Bhandari, and they know we're safe here, so that'll buy us more time. I just texted them that you can't get enough of the library, Giada, so we might be a little slow getting back."

"Okay," I say, uncertainly. I feel a little bad, lying to the Calamoneris and getting them so worried, but magical creatures' lives are on the line.

Moss digs in his backpack for something and pulls out his earbuds, asking, "Is it okay if I wear these while we work? Feeling a little iffy today. Music helps."

I smile. "Sure thing."

Moss puts in his earbuds while Fe settles on his shoulder, cooing softly. Sinistro sits on the edge of the table between Jodi and me, careful not to stand on our notes.

Time blazes by as we continue to research in relative quiet. Every now and then, one of us will pop up from our notes to share an idea or read a passage from a book. Sometimes, we'll stop and eat some snacks, pace the rows of books, or go to the bathroom. The magical sun moves ever lower in the enchanted sky. I keep my phone on the table, checking every so often to see if Alessia's called or texted. My magic twists and turns in my belly. I can't tell if my imagination's making me think that it's not as strong as yesterday or if it really, truly isn't. I squeeze my eyes shut and grip my cornicello, too afraid to confront the reality of the bargain I made with Angie.

After a long stretch of silence, Moss perks up and removes his earbuds, his eyes wide. "I figured out the business card and how to contact the guy!"

Jodi clasps her hands together, bouncing up on her toes. "What do we need to do?"

Moss turns his book to face us and points at a long paragraph followed by a diagram on the next page. "It's this ancient technique used by witches in the sixteenth century. Mary Tudor, the English queen, invented it."

Jodi and I read the page that details what we'll need to call upon the person whose name is on the card: a mirror, candle, and dark room. Using the candle, you burn the card to ash and chant the person's name however many times it says on the card. If you do all those things, then the person will appear in the mirror's reflection, and you can talk to them.

"Like Bloody Mary?" Jodi asks, an eyebrow arched. "We say this guy's name seventeen times and he'll pop up in the mirror?"

"Exactly like that." Moss nods. "Let's find a place to call him."

"You may want to disguise yourselves," Sinistro adds. He stretches out his back, his tail curling into a question mark. "If this man knows you're just kids, he won't take you seriously."

"That's a good point," I say to Sinistro before turning back to Moss and Jodi. "We need to come up with a plan first."

"Oooh, I love a good plan," Jodi says, her eyes wide as she looks between us. "The Streghe del Malocchio are excellent planners."

"First, we need to find a quiet, dark room with a mirror and some candles." I lean closer to Moss and Jodi, my voice a whisper. We huddle together over our table. Pages flutter, books slam shut, and overhead the lights flicker on and off as magic twists through the air. Low voices of students studying at the tables around us harmonize with our own as if joining together in a chant. The library's magic pushes and pulls against our own, building and cascading as our plan takes form.

Moss, Sinistro, Fe, and I are crammed into a tiny bathroom where we found a mirror hanging above a leaky sink. Jodi's standing guard outside just in case anyone ignores the out-of-service sign we stuck on the door and tries to come in anyway. After our conversation about the Madre's possible true intentions, and Jodi's relationship with the Streghe del Malocchio, my heart's softened toward her. She wasn't exactly suspicious, just misunderstood.

We snuck over to the lost and found box, taking some long-forgotten hats—one an old dusty gray fedora and the other a floppy sun hat—and sweaters as makeshift disguises. The fedora's too big for Moss's head and slips over his eyebrows. Paired with the bright blue and neon green sweatshirt he tugged over his Yankees T-shirt, he looks like a funny old nonno.

"We don't know where this hat's been," Moss grumbles. "It could have lice for all we know."

I can't stifle the laugh that bubbles up from my throat. Moss throws me a glare and crosses his arms over his chest, saying, "Yeah, yeah, yeah. At least I don't look confused about the weather. The sun hat and ugly Christmas sweater don't match at all."

I just laugh harder, clutching my sides and giggling until my belly aches. Finally, after a moment, my laughter slows and I wipe a tear from my eye, leaning against the cool tiled wall. "Okay, let's be serious now."

"I've been trying to for the past five minutes." Moss rolls his eyes.

Another bout of laughter threatens to explode out of me, but I'm able to bite this one back. I hold up the candle we found in a custodian's closet and Moss carefully lights it. Fe flicks the light switch off with her wing and the room goes dark, the candle casting long shadows on the walls. Moss pulls Joe Lombardo's business card from his pocket, its gold rim glinting in the winking candlelight.

"You ready?" Moss asks.

I nod, the adrenaline pumping through my veins making it hard to speak. I can feel Sinistro pressed against my leg and take a deep breath.

Moss touches the card's edge to the flame. The smell of burning paper fills the small space and magic hangs in the air like humidity, heavy and almost suffocating. We stand in silence until the entire card's been devoured by the fire. Ash stains Moss's fingertips.

"Are you ready?" I ask, my voice raspy and raw.

"I am. Are you?" Moss counters, something like fear in his eyes. An expression that probably matches my own.

For the second time, I nod and we both face the mirror, the candlelight looming over our faces and distorting them with shadows. I grab Moss's hand and he squeezes mine as we begin to chant Joe Lombardo's name.

We chant *one, two, three, four, five* times.

The flame blinks rapidly as if caught in a storm. Wax weeps from the candle and burns my hand. Magic swirls in the mirror, our reflections warping and reforming in the glass.

Six, seven, eight, nine, ten times.

Anxiety pools in my stomach, threatening to drown me from the inside out. I grip Moss's hand tighter and feel Sinistro wrap his tail around my leg.

Eleven, twelve, thirteen, fourteen, fifteen, sixteen times.

Sweat drips down the back of my neck as the room gets hotter, more bogged down with a strange, ancient magic. Our reflections are gone as the mirror's now completely obscured by thick, gray clouds. I can feel my own magic responding to the strange magic in the air. It curls around my bones and hides behind my heart, unsure of the magic in the mirror. I dig my nails into Moss's hand and resist the urge to close my eyes.

Seventeen times.

The flame snuffs out and the bathroom smells like smoke. We stand in total darkness, hands clasped, the only sound our ragged breathing. Madonna mia. Leave it to Bloody Mary to come up with the scariest way possible to communicate with other witches.

A faint light pulses along the mirror's perimeter. Suddenly, the clouds shift, and one shadow stands out among the others. It starts to take the shape of a man. At first, it's fuzzy, but then the lines begin to sharpen, and his features start coming into view. Slicked back hair and broad shoulders. A pointed chin. However, his eyes are still obscured and it's hard to make out the other details of his face. Even though it's frustrating that we can't see him fully, it's a relief to know that maybe he's unable to see us, too. Hopefully he can't tell we're just kids.

"Who's there?" A low voice with a heavy New York accent calls from the mirror. The shadow shifts as he leans in closer.

"Uhh…" I clear my throat, trying to make my voice seem older. "Ciao, Joe."

"It's *Lucky* Joe," he says, and I roll my eyes. "What do you need?"

"What a charmer," Sinistro whispers.

"Excuse you," I snap. "There's no need to be rude."

Moss elbows me in the side and says in a fake deep voice, "My associate and I are interested in learning more about your business. We're guaritori, you see, and any new avenues in magical medicine are intriguing to us. We'd like to learn more about the medicines you're inventing and possibly find a way that we can help your organization."

Joe's quiet for a moment. A strange song, like a music box, floats out from the mirror as he considers Moss's offer. I strain to focus on the tune, but it's hard to hear as there are other noises like muffled chatter and people laughing overlapping with it.

Finally, Joe speaks again. "Alright…we could use the

help of guaritori. The ones we've approached so far have all refused us."

"I wonder why," Sinistro scoffs and I nudge him gently to remind him to keep quiet.

"Maybe because you kidnapped—" Moss elbows me again and this time pairs it with a sharp look. I cough to cover my mistake. "I mean to say, we're interested in working with a unicorn. Do you have any leads?"

"You wanna meet the unicorn?" Joe asks, suspicion in his tone. "Why would you wanna see the unicorn?"

I'm listening to him very closely, ready to pick up on any clue or misstep, and I hear it: *the* unicorn. He said *the* and not *a*, like he has one in mind, like he has one ready. He has our baby unicorn. Anger stabs me in the belly, and I dig my fingernails into my palms to resist the urge to give Joe a piece of my mind. He has such little regard for all magical creatures. Madonna mia, I hate this. If it wasn't obvious before, clearly Joe Lombardo's a fool.

Before I can speak, Moss answers smoothly, "Yes. We have our own reasons, as guaritori, for wanting to work with a unicorn. And if you truly have one in your possession, we'll know your business is real."

"Huh. I guess that makes sense," Joe says.

"Of course it does," I mutter.

BANG! BANG! BANG!

192

A booming knock fills the tiny bathroom, making Moss and me jump.

"What was that?" Joe asks. "Is someone else there?"

"Erm…we're just getting some interference. Can we meet you in an hour?"

BANG! BANG! BANG!

"I don't know. Something's up with you two… How'd you get my business card to call me anyhow?"

The music box song cuts through the awkward silence and it sounds so familiar, but I can't place it.

BANG! BANG! BANG!

"You're up to some kind of funny business." Joe shifts in the mirror and his profile starts to get fainter. The shadows begin to hide him from us.

"Wait—" I yell.

"Hey!" A man busts in through the door, colliding with Moss and Fe, who then bump into Sinistro and me. The bathroom's filled with light and I squint against the brightness, completely disoriented. "What're you doing in here? This bathroom's out of service."

"I tried to stop him," Jodi yells, following the man, who looks to be a custodian with his coveralls and mop.

"Did you call Joe?" she says, her voice full of hope.

I look back at the mirror, but all I see are my own wide

eyes, sweaty hair, and frizzy curls. Joe's gone and replaced with our reflections.

Moss drags me past the confused custodian and out of the bathroom, Sinistro hurrying behind us. We rush to the foyer, through the entryway, and end up back out in front of the New York Public Library. I sit on the steps to catch my breath, tearing off the sun hat and sweater. Sinistro hops into my lap and nuzzles his head against my cheek. The sun's starting to set behind the buildings, the sky painted warm golds, pinks, and purples. I can smell sugary nuts being heated up in a cart nearby mixing with the scent of asphalt from the hot pavement. Cars honk their horns and people walk by talking away on their phones.

Everything's a blur except for Sinistro's whiskers tickling my face. I take a deep breath to calm my nerves, but my hands won't stop shaking. Tears press against my eyelashes and the anger I felt for Joe grows into a full-blown rage.

"ARGH!" I scream, dragging my fingers through my messy ponytail. "We don't have any more clues. We're freakin' stuck at a dead end. AGAIN. He's gonna hurt the unicorn and there's nothing we can do to stop him and his stupid organization." The tears fall hot down my face, and I scrub at them. "They're gonna keep hurting more and more magical creatures. It's never gonna end."

"Giada," Sinistro says softly. "We're not going to give up. We haven't before and we've faced worse than this."

I hug him tighter and plant a big kiss between his ears, my tears soaking his fur.

"I'll let you have that one kiss because you're sad," he adds and I laugh, wiping my nose with the back of my hand.

"I just don't want to let any creatures down, you know?"

"I know. And you won't. You haven't yet. We just need to come up with a plan."

"How're we gonna find him when we don't have any idea where he is? The mirror barely showed any of his face."

Sinistro hops from my lap to snuggle into my side as I bury my head in my hands, a headache forming just behind my eyes. Someone begins to whistle. A cheery tune that collides with my sour mood like a runaway train. I look up and it's Moss, whistling as he rummages through his bag for some water and snacks to refuel. The song he's whistling is *so* familiar. It bounces around my brain, trying to find purchase on a memory. And then it hits me. I jump up from the steps and ask, "What is that song? How do you know it?" ·

Moss stares at me and nods. "It's the Central Park carousel song. It got stuck in my head, but I don't know why."

Excitement sparks in my veins. "That's the circus-y song that was playing when Joe was talking to us!"

Moss jumps up, drops his bag on the steps, and pumps his fist in the air. "No dead ends here! We're gonna save the unicorn!" He throws his arms around me in a hug, and Jodi stands off to the side, unsure of whether to join us or not. I know it's because of me.

"C'mon, Jodi," I say, holding an arm out to her.

After a moment, she joins us in our group hug, unable to keep the smile from her face. "Let's go now!"

Sinistro leaps onto my shoulder and, with a renewed energy, we find the closest subway station and take the train uptown to Central Park.

13

By the time we emerge from the subway station near Central Park, the sun has already sunk far below the buildings and nighttime has pooled over the sky like the depths of the Mediterranean Sea. It's hard to see the stars in Manhattan, but I can feel their magic strengthening mine. And even though we can't see many of the stars, the moon's brilliant and round and glowing—her pale light shining down on us and reinforcing our magic with its own. I can feel Diana in its radiance.

We rush down twisting lanes and under steep bridges, our feet splashing through puddles and pounding against bricks. It's chilly as the last bits of winter cling to the evening air but sweat still collects on the back of my neck and under my arms. I'm glad I wore jeans today and applied an extra layer of my anti-chafing salve after my shower this morning. Chubby thighs and running around Central Park don't mix.

There's hardly anyone in the park this late and those that are don't seem to pay us any mind. Most are on their way out as night begins to set in. As we make our way deeper into the park, however, it seems like the animals begin to take over. Bats zoom in and out of the trees, rabbits dart across the expansive lawns, and birds squawk from branches. But then something catches my eye and I think it's another rabbit when I notice horns jutting out of its head. It joins a band of other horned rabbits sitting between two overgrown bushes. I slow my pace and grab Moss's arm to get his attention. Jodi and Sinistro stop running, too, and Fe lands on Moss's shoulder. Moss raises an eyebrow at me as I put a finger up to my lips.

"Jackalopes," I whisper, nodding over to the animals. The others follow my line of sight and spy them, too.

"I didn't know jackalopes came this far north," Moss says, taking his phone out to snap a picture. "Incredible."

Just as we're about to move on, we see fish fluttering over a small pond. But unlike traditional flying fish, these ones aren't just gliding. They're flying above the water like dragonflies or birds, their scaly wings glinting in the moonlight.

"The park comes to life at night—all the magical animals must feel safe here," Jodi says.

"Well, maybe they did," I reply, looking up at the trees and scanning the bushes for any more creatures. "But now that there's a poacher lurking around the carousel, who knows?"

Just as we're about to move on, a pack of what reminds me of the winged monkeys from *The Wizard of Oz* begins circling overhead. Their skin is gray and leathery, their wings expanding the length of at least one or one and a half taxicabs. They zoom down from the sky and land in front of us. Some of these creatures have horns, while others have large wrinkles in their foreheads. They're fascinating to look at and don't feel like typical animals. Looking at the precision of some of their features, it seems as if they were formed by artists and not nature.

And then it hits me. Madonna mia. These aren't just any creatures. These are gargoyles. It's different seeing them move, dipping down gracefully from the sky and stretching out in front of us. There's no hint of them being born from stone.

I tilt my head, assessing them. Two of them have giant ears, nearly as big as their wings. And another has those familiar pebbly eyes and horns. They look like the gargoyles from Angie's building.

"Uhh…ciao, gargoyles." I take a step forward in front of Sinistro, Moss, Jodi, and Fe. My arms tense but I leave them hanging at my sides, palms open, to show I'm not holding on to anything threatening. I feel my magic swirling through my body and electrifying in my veins. If I can get one of the gargoyles to trust me enough, I can try communicating with them.

But then the largest one—the gargoyle with two small horns sticking out from his forehead—moves forward. His mouth twists into what I think is meant to be a smile but looks more like a grimace. And then, to my complete surprise, he speaks.

"Hello, little human. We don't mean to frighten you." His voice is like gravel under a boot, a rasp of rocks and stones.

"You can talk?" I say, head tilted to the side.

"Of course we can talk," he responds simply. "When our mother made us, she gifted us with the ability to speak. All creators do so."

"So cool," I can hear Moss say from behind me. And I have to agree. It's amazingly awesome the kind of power magical builders possess. It must take a super powerful strega to create gargoyles. Once all this is over, I'm gonna read as much as I can about them.

"You must've found us for a reason," I say. "What can we do for you?"

"We're the gargoyles from the building you flew onto earlier today. We overheard your conversation with Angie. You protect creatures."

"We do." I take a few steps forward, craning my neck to get a look at all the gargoyles. "Is there something you need?"

Another gargoyle waddles up. It's smaller and has a tiny mouth filled with sharp, stony teeth, and just one eye perched right above its nose like a cyclops. Atop the gargoyle's lumpy head, it looks like it should have a horn—however, bits of crumbling rock surround its base.

"I was attacked," the gargoyle says in a small, squeaky voice. "Last night, when we were out hunting for food, a man tried to snatch me away from my family."

Jodi gasps. "No...could it be...?" She locks eyes with Moss and me, her mouth in a grim line.

Anger rolls over my bones like thunder and I clench my hands into fists. Behind me, Moss communicates with Fe, whistling back and forth. I feel Sinistro brush up against my leg as he lets out a little howl.

"I'm pretty sure we know who," I say.

"It wasn't the first time this has happened either," the larger gargoyle adds. "We've heard rumors of someone

201

taking magical creatures. Stealing them from all over the city and doing terrible things to them."

"And he hurt you?" Moss asks through clenched teeth, his gaze on the smaller gargoyle. I can hear the fury in his voice, and it adds to my own. Our magic bounces off one another in a cacophony.

The gargoyle shakes its head. "I rammed my horn into his leg and then started shouting for the others. That's how it broke off."

"So, can you help us?" the larger gargoyle asks. "I know you have ties to the Jersey Devils and helping us might be seen as a betrayal of the New Jersey magical creatures—"

"We don't take sides. We help *all* creatures. Especially creatures mistreated by terrible, monstrous humans. Madonna mia," I say, before he can go any further.

"But what about the unicorn?" Jodi asks. "We don't have a lot of time."

I look over my shoulder at her and then back at the gargoyles. Time is of the essence, but a magical vet doesn't leave any animal behind. "We need to help them. We can't leave any creature injured. We can work fast."

Jodi nods and asks the gargoyles, "Did you happen to get a good look at him?"

"He had slick black hair and was wearing a three-piece

suit like he was going to a fancy restaurant," the gargoyle replies.

"He needs to be stopped," Moss grumbles.

"Do you know him?" the larger gargoyle asks.

"*Of* him," Moss clarifies.

"He kidnapped a unicorn," I say as I tug off my backpack and zip it open with more force than I intended. I begin rummaging through the supplies I packed, adding, "We're on our way to deal with him."

"Please stop him," the larger gargoyle says. "We can't have him hurting us or others. There are already so few of us."

My magic ebbs and flows, its inconsistency making me nervous. It feels much stronger than it did earlier, and I wonder if this means that Alessia could have found Angie's purse by now. But still I don't know if it's stable enough for me to heal the gargoyle. It might be too temperamental right now to control. I chew on my lip, hands shaking as doubt starts to twist through me. It doesn't matter, though—I need to try.

I pull out a salve and Moss puts a hand on my wrist. "I want to try."

"I can help you," I begin to say, though I'm grateful for the chance to let my magic recuperate for a bit longer, but Moss shakes his head.

"I want to do it. With Fe. As much as I appreciate your help, I want to prove to myself that I can do it. You said so yourself that field experience is better than just practice." Moss shrugs, adding, "Besides, you need to conserve your energy for when we rescue the unicorn."

"Please be careful. If you start feeling sick or that you're pushing too much, remember I'm here to help."

Moss nods and walks over to the smaller gargoyle's side, gently placing a hand on its shoulder. "I'm Moss," he says. "And my bird's name is Ofelia, but we call her Fe. We're going to help you."

The gargoyle nods and sits on the ground as Moss kneels before him and unzips his backpack. He pulls out a jar, a long strand of ivy or some kind of plant, an emerald, a hematite, and what looks like a portable heating pad. "I've got a few things here. It might not seem like much, but I know I can get the job done."

I can't help but grin at Moss's bedside manner. He reminds me so much of Mr. Calamoneri with his calming presence and consistent reassurance. He's a natural, just like his dad.

"First things first, this is a heating pad. I use it when my stomach's cramping really bad. Are you feeling any pain or stiffness? The warmth will help with that."

The gargoyle nods slowly, inching just a bit closer. Moss

turns on the heating pad and carefully places it on the gargoyle's head. Then, he opens the jar and shows its contents to the gargoyle. "This is a simple restorative potion called Marrow Mend. It's made from field bindweed, moonlight cactus, and drool from a three-headed dog's center head. We can only make it under a new moon."

I lean in, interested in the concoction. "How were you able to get the drool?"

"Mom has a friend in New Orleans that has a three-headed dog. She gives us buckets full of drool in exchange for potions."

He holds up the plant and continues, "What we're gonna do is reattach the horn with this blooming field bindweed and I'll thread the emerald and hematite through it. The emerald will encourage growth and the hematite sucks out all the negative energy—it'll also boost protection. Then, once the horn is in place, you'll drink the Marrow Mend. I'll also say a spell to strengthen the crystals and help the healing process."

"Will I taste the drool?" the gargoyle asks, his mouth twisted into a grimace.

Moss laughs, shaking his head. "It sounds gross, but the drool's almost as tasteless as water."

The gargoyle visibly relaxes and hands the horn over to Moss who gets right to it. Jodi stands beside me, her eyes wide as she watches. "Madre would be fascinated by this. She loves studying how other witches work."

"It's pretty clever, yeah?" I pull my veterinarian's log out of my bag, unable to resist taking notes, and quickly begin jotting down what Moss is doing. "I've never heard of field bindweed. My family's bone healing potion's so different from his. Even the crystals aren't something I use often, but maybe I should. They've got a ton of helpful properties."

It's impressive watching Moss. I think back to the day before yesterday, when Mr. Calamoneri and I walked in on him practicing with Fe. How frustrated Moss was that his potion wasn't working. And here he is now, helping mend this gargoyle's horn.

Fe hops from Moss's head to his left shoulder, her head tilted and black beady eyes flashing with interest as he carefully reattaches the horn and winds the field bindweed around it. Moss then slips the crystals into the bindweed, making sure they both touch the horn. As he's about to feed the gargoyle the Marrow Mend, he hesitates and looks back at me.

"Next is the spell," he says.

"I don't know the spell you plan on casting."

"It's for the crystals. The spell will charge them, making

them work faster," Moss explains. "Okay," he sighs and cracks his knuckles. "I'm gonna get to work."

I take a few steps back to give Moss and Fe some room. I watch Moss as he closes his eyes and takes a deep breath through his nose and holds it for a few seconds before slowly exhaling from his mouth. I know he's taking the time to prepare himself to do magic in his own way, using the breathing exercises his therapist taught him. I think it's pretty cool. He does this a few more times before rubbing his hands together and touching his fingertips to the crystals pressed against the gargoyle's horn. Fe flaps her wings slowly, cooling the sweat beading on Moss's forehead. And then, he begins to mutter the words to his spell.

"I call upon the earth and stars
The energy swirling through the air
Mend this creature, make him whole
Protect him with my magic's care."

At first there seems to be nothing. Moss readjusts his hold on the crystals and says the spell again. He rolls his shoulders. Anticipation winds its way up my spine and I stand up straighter, craning my neck to get a better view of the crystals. Next to me, Jodi worries her lip and shifts from foot to foot. Still nothing.

Moss runs a hand through his hair and grumbles something under his breath. Fe hops onto his other shoulder, twittering something in his ear. When Moss shakes his head in response, Fe whistles again, this time louder. Fe jumps onto the gargoyle's shoulder and nuzzles her head against the horn. Finally, after a moment, Moss nods and begins his breathing exercises again—slowly through his nose, holding for ten seconds, and releasing through his mouth. He places his fingertips on the crystals once more, saying the spell again, this time slower, making sure to breathe as he goes—and that's when I feel it. Moss's magic crackles through the air. Then, the crystals flicker.

Jodi jumps and nudges me in the side. "Did you see that?" she asks in a hushed voice.

I nod, a smile spreading over my lips—so wide my face hurts.

The crystals flicker again, but this time their light stays consistent. They shine a brilliant green and black, shimmering across Moss's face. He leans back, eyes wide as he sees his magic in action. Fe flies into the air and circles just above the gargoyle and Moss. As she does, the magic in the air grows stronger, thrumming like a heartbeat. The gargoyle's horn glows, and the crystals fall from its sides. The horn's reattached, no longer a crumbling mess. Moss pumps his fist in the air, a bark of laughter escaping his lips.

He takes out his water bottle and drinks deeply. When he puts the bottle down, there's a thoughtful look on his face.

It's great seeing him access his magic by doing things in his very own way.

"Here," I say, grabbing a bag of pretzels from my backpack. I take a few for myself before tossing them to him. "Make sure to eat something, too."

I turn to the gargoyle. "How do you feel?"

The gargoyle tilts his head slowly to the side. "At first it felt really warm," he says. "And now I feel this tingling from my toes all the way up to my horn. I can feel my horn again. It's back!" He looks at Moss, his eye wide as he smiles. "Thank you, thank you, thank you!"

Moss stands, shaking the gargoyle's hand blearily. "Thank *you*! I'm so happy that I could help."

"We won't forget your generosity," the larger gargoyle says. "You've helped a member of our family. We are in your debt."

"Oh, no worries. It's my duty to help," Moss explains, the sleepy smile still plastered on his face.

"And we're gonna make sure something like this doesn't happen again." I pull my backpack straps higher onto my shoulders and begin hurrying down the path again. "Sorry to leave so soon, but we need to save a unicorn."

Moss and Jodi wave their goodbyes, chasing after me and Sinistro as we hurry under another bridge. Fe flies overhead and, behind me, Moss munches on the pretzels as we run. My heart pounds against my ribs and all I can think about is the unicorn. I push harder, run faster, as the exhaustion gives way to rage, which turns into fear. I hope we're not too late. We can't be too late. Not just for the unicorn. The lives of all these magical creatures depends on us.

14

"We're almost there," Jodi calls over her shoulder. Moss, Sinistro, Fe, and I are only a few steps behind as we follow Jodi to the carousel. It's completely dark now and a chill settles in the air, freezing the sweat on the back of my neck and making me shiver.

After we hurry up a small hill, I hear it: the song from the bathroom at Moss's school. It's faint, but that circus-y music is unforgettable. Excitement squeezes in my chest and I pick up my pace.

Moss and I nearly collide with Jodi as she comes to a dead stop at the top of the hill. Hidden under a brick gazebo is the carousel. It shines out from between the columns and casts ghostly shadows over the grounds. The red, gold, and green lights beckon like a lighthouse, calling us to shore. I resist the urge to run down the hill, screaming my head off for the unicorn.

I look to the others and ask, "What's the plan?"

"What? I thought you had one," Moss says, his eyebrows raised.

"Nope."

"Well…huh."

"Giada," Sinistro begins. "Does that shadow look strange to you?"

"What shadow?" I ask.

His tail sticks straight up and puffs out like a feather boa. I follow his glare and see a small shed a few feet to the right. A tall figure steps onto the path near the carousel and is backlit, his face obscured. He has a bit of a limp in his left leg and appears to carry a cane. I nudge Moss and Jodi, nodding toward the man.

"Do you think that's Joe?" Jodi whispers.

"It has to be him," I say, squinting as if I can somehow see through the darkness. "Who else would be lurking around the carousel at night?"

"He might have an accomplice with him," Moss suggests. "And if that's the case then we need to be extra careful."

"Let's wait here a bit? Scope him out and see if anyone's coming." Jodi kneels on the grass next to Sinistro and places her bag carefully at her side. Moss does the same and takes a minute to get some water. I look between them and Joe, weighing the option of just storming up to him with all my fury against the danger of there being another person (or persons) in the area. Joe moves closer to the carousel, walking the perimeter and disappearing behind it.

Finally, with a huff of annoyance, I sit down and cross my arms over my chest. "Fine," I grumble. "But let's not wait too long. Only long enough to make sure it's safe."

"Do you honestly think a group of kids and two familiars confronting a man that's trying to kidnap magical creatures is ever gonna be safe?" Moss asks, giving me a look of disbelief. "Jeez, we're in way over our heads here. More than I originally thought."

"Don't get cold feet now!" I shout. "We need to save the unicorn. We're so close!"

"First of all, *be quiet*. He could hear us," Moss warns. "Second of all, I'm not getting cold feet, but it probably would've been smarter to have adults with us."

"Adults can't fix everything." I shrug, adding, "Besides, I saved my brother, Alessia, my zia, and my parents without the help of any adults."

"But how much sooner would you have saved everyone

if you had more help?" Moss glances at Joe and shakes his head. "I get that you had Alessia and Sinistro and they're great, but we don't know what we're dealing with here."

"Well, we can't turn back now." I stand up, hands planted on my hips. "We have to act. Who knows if we'll get this opportunity again!"

"*Shhh!*" Jodi and Moss hush me at the same time.

"Hey! Who's there?" a familiar, gruff voice calls out. Joe's shadowed figure is back in front of the carousel and—even though I can't see his face—I can feel his eyes darting across the hill.

Fear unfurls in my body like a spider's long legs, dragging over every raw nerve. I cover my mouth with my hands and dive for the ground. I think about how unpredictable my magic has been and wonder if I'll be able to count on it for what lies ahead. But it's too late. Joe's spotted us and is rushing up the hill.

Gripping my cornicello in my fist, I scramble to my feet. Sinistro stands in front of me, his hair electrified with his magic and sticking up in all directions. Moss and Jodi leap up next to me, Jodi's hands clenched in fists and Moss standing tall with Fe on his shoulder. They look brave, ready to fight, but their anxiousness shows in little tells. In Jodi moving from one foot to the other. In Moss fidgeting with his backpack straps. I'm not better off. My heart plummets into my stomach like a free-falling elevator. I swallow hard, my hands shaking.

And before we can scream, Joe's standing right in front of us. From this close, I can make out his caterpillar eyebrows and the bump in his nose. His thin lips are set in an unamused expression that reminds me of the one Maestra Vita wore anytime I fell asleep in class. There's a bit of stubble on his pointed chin and bags under his eyes. Both contrast sharply with his pale white skin and make it look like he hasn't slept in days. In his left hand is a cane, its top decorated with a silver dragon head.

"A little late for three kids to be roaming Central Park by themselves, isn't it?" Joe asks, twisting a ring on his right pinkie finger.

I square my shoulders and tamp down my twisting nerves. Now's not the time to clam up. Before Joe can stop me, I shove past him and run down the hill—Moss, Jodi, Fe, and Sinistro at my heels.

"Hey!" I hear him call. "What're you doing?"

"We're rescuing the unicorn you stole," I yell over my shoulder. I skid to a stop in front of the carousel, bracing my hands against the gold railing. The carousel's near-deafening jaunty organ music booms against my eardrums.

"Giada!" Sinistro shouts over the noise. "Giada, look at the animals!"

Amid the traditional horses and carriages decked out in flowers and jewels are animals not typically found on a carousel. A small jackalope, frozen in place with a gold rod through its back. A phoenix, its red and orange wings immobile in the air, moving up and down with the music. Then, as the carousel spins, I spot a familiar creature. A Jersey Devil with its leathery wings outstretched and its mouth open in a silent scream. And right next to it is the unicorn. Her long, beautiful horn puncturing the night sky like a beacon of light. Her luxurious mane adorned with purple and yellow flowers.

My hands shake against the railing, and I follow around the carousel. Bile rushes up my throat and I clutch my neck, swallowing the sickness down.

"Oh, my goodness. He's hidden them in plain sight," Jodi whispers, her voice trembling. "How do we save them?"

Moss peers around before pointing at something in the center and saying, "Look. There's a lever. We can at least stop the carousel and then figure out how to free them."

"I'll try getting to it," Jodi says. She slips underneath the railing and scrambles onto the carousel, stumbling onto her knees as it jolts her forward.

"Do you like my menagerie?" Joe yells over the music. "We're building something special."

I whip around, fists hanging at my sides, fixing Joe in a glare. "What did you do to them?"

"They aren't dead." Joe shakes his head, tapping his cane on the brick walkway. "Just…sleeping. Frozen in time like a mosquito in amber."

"But they won't be alive for long, will they?" Moss says. "You're using them to make medicine."

"I'm merely a middleman for an organization of witches—C&C Medicinals—who *are* making medicine. They call me the hunter," Joe says with a smirk.

Behind him, Jodi fumbles with the lever. She tugs at it, straining with all her might to shut off the carousel. Her foot slips and she falls onto her backside with a thunk. Joe squints at the noise and is about to turn around when I scream.

"Do you know how irresponsible it is to take these magical creatures?" I snap, tears collecting in my eyes.

"You don't seem to understand that this—" he extends his arms, dark eyes reflecting the carousel's light "—is bigger than just me."

"You're part of it, though," Moss yells.

"But what's so wrong with making medicine for the masses? Think of all the lives that will be saved. This," Joe says, arching an eyebrow, his fingers gently caressing the cane's dragon head, "is just a taste of what we can do. Isn't it a noble pursuit?"

217

Of course, companies that make medicine are important. People need medications and vaccines. But helping some lives at the cost of others just can't be the only way. I remember what Jodi said about the conversation Joe had with the Madre. About how he was trying to get her to convince other Streghe del Malocchio covens to steal magical creatures. I don't know just how deep this organization goes, but it doesn't matter. What they are doing isn't noble. It's flat-out wrong.

"We've heard what you're trying to do and it's not ethical. Making your operation bigger could wipe out all the magical creatures in the world. Which means no way to collect their hair or feathers or nails or whatever *safely* and with their consent, to make potions and other things to help people. I don't think any of us want that, including you." My breathing comes in hard gasps. A headache forms at the back of my skull and it's taking all my willpower not to shove Joe. "Guaritori and other streghe should only take what is voluntarily given to them by these creatures. It's about respect. That's why there's very little magic in poached ingredients."

"I'm someone who could use medicine like that," Moss begins, his face twisted with anger. "But not at this cost. It's too dangerous. Too drastic. What'll the people you help with the medicine do once it's all dried up? What'll they do if they can't afford to buy overpriced medicine from you anymore? Giada's right—this plan isn't built to last forever."

Joe leans back, eyes assessing me from head to toe. "Some of you witches are so self-righteous and unwilling to share your magic with the non-magical." He tsks in the most obnoxious way. "I'm fortunate to have been contacted by these real witches who understand the importance of spreading the wealth."

"Madonna mia. You don't get it!" I stomp my foot on the ground, magic building in my belly. "If you destroy these creatures, we have *nothing*. We can't help *anyone*. What's this company's plan once all the creatures are dead?"

"That's none of your concern." He shakes his head, a grimace spreading over his face. Then he pauses and I follow his gaze down to Sinistro. "What a handsome cat." He looks up at Moss's shoulder where Fe is perched and taps his cane again. "And a lovely bird. I suppose they aren't all that ordinary. Are they?"

Heat radiates through my blood and burns my cheeks. I squeeze my fists so tight I can feel my nails digging into my skin. I stand in front of Sinistro, sneering at Joe. My voice is low as I warn, "Don't even look at them."

"Hmm. Struck a nerve, eh?"

My magic boils up from my stomach and flows through my veins. It sizzles along the hairs on my arms and the back of my neck, crackling through the curls on top of my head. I can feel the energy from the stars and moon fueling my magic, but what I need now requires more than their help.

I need Diana.

Diana, I think, trying to clear my mind and focus entirely on the goddess, *Diana, goddess of wild animals, please grant me your aid in defending your most vulnerable creatures. We need your help, your strength, in guiding our magic.*

A lightness swirls up inside me. It's like silk slipping between my fingers or the wind tickling across my cheeks. But then it builds, strengthening inside me and blending with my magic.

Moss looks at me from the corner of his eye and mutters, "Do you feel something?"

A grin spreads over my face and I give him a short nod before turning back to Joe. "Are you sure you don't want to let these creatures go?"

"Why would I want to do a thing like that?"

"Because you'll be sorry if you don't."

"Will I?" Joe slams his cane onto the ground and the dragon's glittery diamond eyes turn a fierce red. "When I've got magic at my fingertips?"

"But I thought you weren't a strega?" I say, doubt laced between my words.

Joe raises his cane high into the air and a bolt of red

magic shoots out of the tip and into the night sky. "I've got all the magic I need from your precious creatures."

"That's where you're keeping their magic?" I gasp. "That's how you're controlling them."

"I like to think of it as *my* magic. At least until I turn it over to my boss—taking a bit of it for myself is my finder's fee." He lowers his cane, pointing its tip at my chest. A sly smile curls over his lips. "Once I'm done with you kids, I'll top it off with the help of your cat and bird."

Magic buzzes at the tip of his cane like flies around garbage and I can feel my own magic surging forward in response. Fear settles between the bones of my spinal cord. I take a step back, my throat dry.

But before he can strike, something knocks him off his feet. Moss stands behind Joe with his hand extended, magic sparking on his fingertips. He looks down at his hand, eyes wide, before looking up at me. "I didn't know I could do *that*."

"What'd you do?" I say, grabbing Moss's hand and yanking him under the railing. Sinistro leaps onto the still-moving carousel and we scurry on after him. Jodi stands with her hands on her hips, glaring at the lever.

Moss shrugs. "I don't know. I was angry and worried he'd hurt you and thought about stopping it. Next thing I know my magic's shooting out of my hand."

"It's Diana," I say, rushing to the unicorn and running a gentle hand over her back. "She's given us a boost so we can save the creatures."

"Help me stop the carousel!" Jodi calls, trying once again to yank the lever.

We run back but, just as we're about to reach her, Joe leaps onto the carousel. He's wobbly on his feet, but quickly gains his composure and fixes us with a seething glare. "You little brats really think you're onto something, don't you?" Joe slams his cane down hard and the carousel's floorboards rise like a giant wave. Moss and Sinistro are quick enough to jump over it, but the wave crashes into me. I'm flung off my feet, my back banging into the corner of a carriage. Pain burns through every muscle in my body, vibrating against my bones. I fall to the floor, groaning and rolling onto my side as the carousel continues to careen around and around. Sinistro nudges my shoulder with his head, and I crawl to a sitting position.

"Are you okay, Giada?" Sinistro asks, his green eyes alert with concern.

"I'm gonna have to be," I mutter. My legs are like jelly as I stumble up to my feet.

Joe swings his cane in an arch, but Moss lands a hit to his side and the cane drops to the ground with a clatter.

"Grab his cane!" Moss yells. Jodi clamors for it, chasing

after the cane as it rolls between two horses. But Joe's faster. He hurries after her and knocks Jodi out of the way to wrap his fingers around the cane.

Joe spins his cane and magic sizzles through the air, circling the carousel. It pings against the lights so hard that a few of them pop. Glass shatters and I cover my head, Sinistro scurrying under a carriage seat, as it falls onto us. Joe swings his cane again and the carousel begins to twirl faster. The wind whips across my face and I struggle to push against it toward Joe. Jodi throws a bolt of black light at Joe, who stumbles into the Jersey Devil before thrusting his cane back at her and launching a flurry of silver flies.

Jodi screams as the swarm of flies buzzes around her face and gets tangled in her hair. She swats at them, fighting against their attack. Joe whips his cane around and a flash of blue jets from its tip, hitting Jodi between her shoulder blades and flinging her off the carousel and into the air.

"Jodi!" I shout, hurrying to the carousel's edge and peering into the darkness. Jodi lands with a crash on the grass. My heart is in my throat and I run, trying to keep her in my sight as the carousel continues to spin at a breakneck speed. "Jodi!" I yell again, my voice raw. "Jodi, are you okay?"

In the dark, I clamor over to her side and place a hand on her shoulder. She's badly bruised and there's a large cut on her forehead. Guilt washes over me as I remember how awful I was to her just because she's a Strega del Malocchio. But she gives me a thumbs-up and smiles. "I'm okay," she says, coughing slightly. "Just a little sore."

"A *little* sore?" I ask, the words coming out with a disbelieving laugh.

"Maybe a lot," she concedes. "Go help Moss. I'll be fine. He needs you!"

I turn around just as Moss ducks to avoid purple light shooting from Joe's cane. It bursts against a column, sending a spray of cement and brick into the air. Giving Jodi one last look, I rush behind the column where Moss is hiding, and watch Joe twirl his cane through the air.

"Ugh," I groan, clutching my forehead. "I'm feeling dizzy."

"Me, too," Moss agrees. "We need to stop the carousel."

Nausea gurgles in my stomach and I take a deep breath so I don't puke all over the place. I shake my head. "We need to get his cane," I shout to Moss. "It's the only way to stop him."

Magic vibrates through my arms and in my fingertips. I can feel Diana's power twisting with my own and I imagine a stampede of deer—one of Diana's favorite animals. I let the magic go and it jolts from my hand. A herd of sparkling, gold deer gallop between the horses and carriages, chasing after Joe.

He trips over his feet and falls to the floor, his cane rolling out of his hand. Moss reaches for it, but Joe's too fast and yanks Moss by the leg.

"Ow!" Moss groans, kicking at Joe.

"Hey, watch it!" Joe yells. He pushes Moss and crawls for the cane just as Sinistro pounces on it. But Joe's quick to snatch the cane from underneath Sinistro, causing him to bowl into a horse. He lets out a little yowl, then hops back up to his feet.

Joe stumbles to his feet and growls, "You think this is fast?" He thrusts his cane into the air and swirls it around above his head. The lights flicker violently, a few more shattering, sending more glass down on us. Shards get in my ponytail, and I shake them out of my curls. And then the carousel spins even faster, nearly rocketing me off my feet. I grab on to a pole to steady myself, the nausea that was building in my stomach now racing its way up my throat. The organ music picks up, its once-happy tune turning sinister.

"Madonna mia, make it stop!" I scream, my grip on the pole slipping. Sinistro takes refuge in one of the carriages, his fur flying back off his face and his green eyes wide. A couple feet behind us, Moss clutches on to one of the frozen jackalope's horns, Fe nested in his hair.

Joe struggles toward us, his suit jacket flapping in the wind and a nasty glint in his eyes. I reach out, the magic pulsing in my hands, and envision hitting Joe square in the chest. But the carousel jerks and I lose my balance. The spell zips over his shoulder.

"I can't focus long enough to hit him," I yell.

Moss tries his own spell, but he can't stop from shaking. His hits the top of the carousel and fizzles out among the lights. Joe pushes a button, and a blade slips out of the bottom of his cane, the metal shining in the remaining light. He looks between Moss and me, a crooked grin spreading over his face.

"This'll do the trick," he says with a cackle.

I look at Moss and see the same terror I'm feeling reflected in his eyes. He takes a step back, careful not to fall. My heart slams against my rib cage and I grip my cornicello. Joe raises his cane. I close my eyes, bracing for the pain of it slicing through my skin.

But the pain never comes.

"What?" Joe mumbles. "No! Stop! Everything's gonna be wrecked," he shrieks. I open my eyes in time to see Joe fall, his cane flying into the air and rolling off the carousel. A swoop of leathery wings cuts through the air. There's terror on Joe's face as he tries to scoot backward, slamming into a carriage.

And from the sky comes a fearsome screech.

15

Gargoyles and Jersey Devils circle through the sky, landing gracefully in front of the carousel. They continue howling and bellowing, so loud they drown out the carousel's
music. From behind them, two beams of light cut through
the dark. And I hear a sound that's all too familiar: a horn
honking incessantly.

A huge neon green convertible skids over the grass,
onto the bricks, and comes to a squealing stop mere feet
from the carousel. My heart soars at the sight of Angie and
Alessia jumping out of the car and marching toward us.

"No, no, no!" Joe's fingers twist in his messy hair. He's
collapsed on the ground, a bruise under his left eye but

otherwise looks unharmed. Just rattled. "No one's supposed to even be here."

"Help me with the lever," Moss yells. I scramble over to him as he grips the lever. "My stomach can't take much more of this. I'm gonna hurl if we can't turn it off," he adds. With a deep breath, I grip it, too, and we both pull, straining against the rusted lever. Sweat slicks my palms and my hands ache from pulling. Finally, after what feels like forever, the lever creaks backward. Moss and I stumble into each other as the carousel comes to an abrupt stop. The music shuts off with a groan, but what's left of the lights continue to blink.

I take deep, gulping breaths. My curls are slicked to my neck and forehead and my mouth's dry, my legs and arms sore from all the exertion. Moss has his hands on his knees, trying to get control of his own breathing. He looks pale, his face glistening with sweat.

"Are you okay?" I ask Moss.

He nods, wiping at his brow. "Better now that we're not spinning." Joe glances at us from the corner of his eye and begins to stand when Moss calls out to him. "Hey! Where do you think you're going?"

I envision a spider's web, one as strong and secure as Tartufo's, and the magic builds in my fingertips once more. I fling the spell at Joe while he's distracted by Moss and it smacks him right in the chest, a shimmering white spider's web pinning him to the carriage.

"Huh," Moss says, eyeing the still-frozen creatures. "I thought stopping the carousel would've freed them."

I look over at the jackalope, still immobile, and shake my head. We must be missing something, but whatever it is I'm unsure.

"Giada!" Alessia calls as she runs up onto the carousel. She throws her arms around me in a bone-crushing hug, squeezing me until I feel like I can't breathe. "Madonna mia! You're safe!"

I pull back, grinning at her, and say, "I'm glad *you're* safe! You traveled through Olde Yorque all on your own." My brow furrows as I look over at Angie. She's holding Ooh La La in one arm while picking up Joe's cane. "How are you with Angie? And how'd you know we were here, anyway?"

"Well, I had to return her purse! I found it, after all." Alessia laughs. "And—the gargoyles! They told Angie what was going on. That you were all in danger."

It's my turn to hug Alessia. Relief settles in my bones, and I feel tears prick at my eyes. Everything could have gone so badly, but Alessia risked her life to make sure I'd get to keep my magic. I take a deep breath, feeling my magic. It was difficult to notice when fighting Joe, but it's no longer pitching around in my belly like a stormy sea.

It's settled and strong. She saved me. I wipe at the tears and say, "You're the best friend in the whole universe."

"I try," Alessia says.

"How'd you do it? How'd you get the purse back?"

"Thankfully Olde Yorque's not as terrifying as Malafi," Alessia says with a shrug. "The Madre wasn't particularly happy that I was still there, but I went back to her again and poured my heart out." Alessia grins. "And I may have struck up a deal with her."

"Alessia! Guaritori can't make deals with Streghe del Malocchio."

"Maybe you've rubbed off on me." She laughs. "But it was an easy one to make. In exchange for the purse, I offered to teach them some soul healing spells. The Madre was very grateful for the lesson. Even though they have the fairies down in Olde Yorque, their streghe get sad without a real sky, too. But the soul healing spells should help with that."

"You're brilliant, Alessia." I hug her again, squeezing maybe a little too tight.

"Hey!" Jodi jogs over to us, leaves stuck in her hair and grass stains on her lilac dress. The cut on her forehead looks nasty. I offer her a handkerchief that I dig out of my backpack and she takes it gratefully. She looks at Alessia and smiles. "I'm Jodi! I'm a Strega del Malocchio in training."

Alessia waves, a smile spreading over her face. "I'm Alessia. It's so nice to meet you. Madre told me all about you. Only good things."

At the mention of her Madre, Jodi wiggles her shoulders in a pleased little dance. After a moment, she gestures to the gargoyles and Jersey Devils, grinning as she says, "Look who saved the day!"

"Glad to see that they've put aside their grudge and decided to work together," Moss says.

"Now we just need to figure out what to do next." I pick a stray bit of glass out of my hair and flick it to the ground.

Sinistro nudges up against my leg and meows, his eyes darting over to Joe, who's struggling against the spider's web, his hair dripping into his eyes. "Maybe you can ask him?"

"I hate kids," Joe grumbles under his breath a few feet to our left. "Lousy, loud, and meddling. Should've never gotten involved in this mess."

I march over to him, hands on hips, and sneer down into his face. "*Kids* just destroyed your plans. Now, tell us how to release the creatures or else."

"You think I'm gonna tell you? Just tell you everything because you asked?" He looks up at me and laughs, a low and obnoxious cackle that makes him sound like a cheesy supervillain. I roll my eyes, anger boiling in my belly. "You and your friends ruined my life, kid. No way am I gonna tell you anything."

"Oh, quit it with that nonsense. The only person who ruined your life is *you*." Angie walks over, twirling Joe's cane in her hand like a baton. Ooh La La prances around behind her as she barks and wags her tail. "I've seen an object like this before," she says, turning her attention to the rest of us. "It's interesting magic. Pretty rare, but I've seen a couple like this at AbracAuctions warehouse in Long Island City. It's a vessel that's used to store magic from other sources. If those sources are alive, which is usually the case, they're drained of their magic and turn to husks like you see here."

I gasp. "That's horrible!"

"But it makes sense to use when transporting often wild magical creatures," Alessia says. "You zap them of their magic, cart them where you need them to go, and give them their magic back only when you need to…" She pauses, eyes wide, and gulps. "Only when you need to gather magical ingredients like hair and toenails and—"

"And brains and eyeballs and hearts!" I cut her off, my anger exploding into a full-blown rage.

"It can be wielded by non-magical people but is usually

used by witches to become more powerful," Angie continues. "Generally, like in this case, it's not used for good."

"What do we do with it?" Jodi asks. "Can the creatures get their magic back?"

"If we break his cane, then all the different threads of magic will go back to their owners," Angie says. "It's not a perfect fix. Depending on how much magic he's used, some creatures might never recover." Without warning, Angie snaps the cane over her knee and a burst of rainbow light shoots into the sky.

We leap back, watching reds, purples, oranges, ceruleans, and chartreuses spin through the air, glittering and shimmering like shooting stars. Joe kicks his feet, face red as he groans about the unfairness of it all. But he can throw the biggest tantrum he wants; I only care about watching the magic fly back to where it belongs.

Ribbons of light flit over to the carousel and dance around the jackalope, Jersey Devil, phoenix, and unicorn. The gold rods in the creatures' backs vanish and they begin to stir, yawning and stretching as if waking from a deep sleep. The Jersey Devil hops off the carousel and walks over to the other Jersey Devils, sniffing around their heads and nuzzling against one with brown spots. There's a small cry from the bushes and the band of jackalopes we saw earlier sit there with their heads tilted to the side. The jackalope that had been trapped on the carousel twitches its ears and scurries off toward the bush, greeting its family with a yowl. Then, the phoenix stretches out its great fiery wings—its feathers blinding in the darkness. It stares at us, its black eyes sharp and curious. The phoenix nods its head toward us before launching into the air, circling overhead, chasing after the magic in tight circles.

Looking back at the carousel, I gasp when I see a collection of red and orange singed feathers sitting in a pile. Phoenix feathers are extraordinarily hard to come by and can be used in a ton of different potions and spells. But before I grab them, I search for the unicorn.

She's more beautiful than I thought she'd be, standing on the carousel by the horses. The Pulaskis said that unicorns five years or younger would have pink horns. Her horn is a deep rose color and so bright against her blindingly white mane. She looks over her shoulder at me and the others, blinking slowly as she takes in the scene.

I hold my hands out and approach her slowly as if she were a raptor or T. rex, afraid that she might get spooked and run away. But the unicorn doesn't move. Rather, she lowers her head in a bow. Her magic's like a light summer breeze—familiar, comfortable, safe—and gently greets my own.

"She's incredible," Moss breathes from next to me. "I've never seen anything like her."

"Isn't she amazing?" I say, dropping to a curtsy in response to the unicorn's bow. "We need to check all the creatures for injuries."

From a few feet away, I hear an annoying laugh. Joe is still stuck to the carriage, the spider's web holding strong. He's snickering to himself, shaking his head as he scoffs, "You think I would've hurt them before transporting them to the facility? I'll have you know I deliver only the highest quality products."

"Products?" I repeat, stomach clenching with anger. "They're animals—living, breathing creatures—*not* products."

"You know…just because you caught me and saved a handful of measly *animals* doesn't mean this is all over. C&C Medicinals is much bigger than you realize."

I roll my eyes. "Blah, blah, blah. You're so annoying."

"Yeah, all you do is talk," Jodi agrees, crossing her arms over her chest.

Alessia glares at him, shaking her head. "You lost. Get over it."

"You were just a pawn. How embarrassing," Moss adds.

"What a buffoon. I'll take care of him." Angie heads back to her car and grabs an emerald dragon skin purse with sparkling gold hardware from the back seat. Enchanted gold snakes slither all around the bag, their delicate gold tongues cutting through the air. I've gotta admit, it's a nice purse—worth making a bargain with me to get it back from Olde Yorque.

Angie rummages through the bag as she walks toward us, Ooh La La close on her heels. "Aha," she says, coming to a stop in front of Joe. She taps her heel against the brick walkway and grins at him, a mischievous glint in her eye. "I know you're not gonna tell us all the details."

"You better believe it, sweetheart," Joe says with a smug smile.

"But you might tell my sister. She's got a talent for loosening people's tongues." Angie pulls a small blue-and-silver jewelry box from her purse and opens it. "See this? You're about to get real familiar with its insides."

Joe eyes it suspiciously. "What do you mean?"

"You'll see." Angie winds up the jewelry box and opens the lid. A soft, dreamlike tune begins to play and a little ballerina in a pink dress spins at its center.

The wind picks up around us and a different magic fills the air. It's strange and feels like the moments before a roller coaster barrels down the first hill and into a loop. The sensation makes me uneasy, and I pick up Sinistro, holding him tight to my chest. Soon, the wind grows more intense, grabbing at my ponytail and shirt, tugging at Sinistro's whiskers.

And then a veil of red glitter creeps over Joe. His eyes widen and he starts kicking his legs in protest. "What's going on?" he demands, a quiver in his voice. "No! What is this?" Soon his feet disappear into the red glitter, then his legs. His hands and arms disappear next, and he's completely consumed until just his terror-filled eyes remain. But they vanish, too, with a resounding *pop*.

The red glitter dissipates into the air and the wind dies down. Angie's laugh cuts above the music and her red lips part in a satisfied grin as she stares down at the jewelry box.

"Where'd he go?" Alessia asks. "Did he get away?"

"Ha! He wishes," Angie says. "He's in a time-out until I can get him to Olde Yorque." She holds out the jewelry box for us to see. Goose bumps rise on the back of my neck, and I blink several times to make sure I'm not seeing things. Down in the jewelry box, spinning right next to the ballerina, is Joe.

"Is he okay?" Alessia's voice is full of concern as she peeks over the jewelry box's edge.

"I don't care," I mumble and feel Alessia nudge me in the side. "Come on, he was trying to kidnap magical creatures. Who knows how many he's already hurt?"

But Angie shakes her head. "He'll be comfortable in here. Not sure how he'll do down below, though."

"You're really gonna go back to Olde Yorque?" I ask. "After all this time?"

"I've been putting it off for long enough." Angie lifts her chin, tapping her acrylic nails along the jewelry box's side. "I need to make things right with my sister. And, if what Joe says is true about this company, the Streghe del Malocchio need to take a stand against them. Otherwise there will be major consequences."

"What do you mean?" Moss questions.

"Something like he described will upend both the magical and non-magical worlds. And as gatekeepers of the scales, it's our job to make sure that doesn't happen."

"Remember, he had already spoken to the Madre," Jodi explains. "He wanted her to convince all the other covens to help kidnap creatures. Possibly drain them of their magic entirely and even kill them. And the Madre said they wouldn't help him. She said she wouldn't help Giada, Moss, and Alessia either, but..." She looks up at the sky as if trying to find the answer. "I think in her own roundabout way she did. She practically gave me Joe's business card and had me follow them. She put the pieces into place, but she played the game from a distance."

Angie presses her lips into a firm line and says, "Well,

then I'm gonna have to convince my sister to get her hands dirty and actually help. Wouldn't be the first time I've done that."

Caw-caw. Caw-caw. Overhead, the phoenix cries into the night sky before landing gently near the gargoyles and Jersey Devils. It shakes out its feathers, the smell of smoke singeing the air.

"We better check all the animals," I say, turning to Moss. "Just in case Joe was lying."

He nods, takes a few generous pulls from his water bottle, and we set to work. Moss goes to inspect the jackalope while I take a look at the Jersey Devil. Despite being trapped without its powers for who knows how long, the Jersey Devil appears to be in good shape. A little tired, but that's to be expected after suffering through everything.

"The jackalope looks alright," Moss says after a brief physical. "No obvious injuries or anything. It just seems relieved to be reunited with its family." He smiles at the band of them while rummaging through his bag. "I'll take a look at the phoenix if you wanna do the same for the unicorn?" He produces a pair of black leather gloves and adds, "I've got these, after all. They'll be helpful against the heat."

Alessia and Sinistro follow me over to the unicorn while Jodi and Angie talk in hushed tones about Madre and

Olde Yorque. The unicorn looks more comfortable than I'd expect for a creature that was just released from captivity.

"She's so gorgeous," Alessia whispers, carefully approaching the unicorn and placing a tentative hand on her side. "I love her already. She makes me feel calm. Safe."

"Unicorns have that effect on us. It's extraordinary magic."

"It really is. I can't wait to bring her to the sanctuary where she'll be protected from poachers like this Joe guy." She nuzzles her head into the unicorn's neck and the unicorn noses her in response. "I'll get to learn all about soul magic from her."

I smile at the pair before beginning my physical assessment of the unicorn, starting with carefully examining her horn for any chips or damage. "Are you sure you're not a magical vet?" I joke as Alessia steps back from the unicorn to let me work.

She laughs and shakes her head. "Pretty sure I'd have met my own Sinistro or Fe by now."

"Well, you're gonna be one of the best guaritrici ever." Alessia beams at me as I move on to checking the unicorn's neck and back muscles before finishing up with an inspection of her legs. I do a second look to ensure there are no wounds or abrasions, but I find none. She looks to be in good health like the Jersey Devil, just fatigued after her ordeal.

"No broken bones or aching muscles. Her magic levels are normal. I'd say she's alright and just needs some rest," I say, planting my hands on my hips. "The sanctuary will be good for her."

"How're we going to get her all the way back to New Jersey anyhow?" Alessia asks, tilting her head as she assesses the unicorn. "She's kind of big and definitely won't fit in the back of Angie's car."

I snort. "As if Angie'd let a unicorn sit in her car. She'd destroy the interior." I look around at the gargoyles and Jersey Devils huddled together near the top of the hill and an idea comes to mind. "Remember how we got here?"

Alessia's eyes widen, and she shakes her head. "No. Absolutely not. There's no way I'm flying over the river on the back of a Jersey Devil again."

"Well, when you were in Olde Yorque, they did help us free a bunch of horses from a stable. They can definitely carry her." I tap my foot on the ground, grinning as I add, "And we can't take a train or bus back with an actual unicorn. Think of the scene that'd cause."

"Giada," Alessia whines. "You know I hate heights."

"I promise it's perfectly safe. You know it is."

After a moment, Alessia sighs and says, "Fine. But you owe me. Big-time."

I laugh in response, and we head over to Moss, who is just wrapping up with the phoenix. "I think we should bring him with us. He seems fine, but he's far away from home. My parents and the Pulaskis can help figure out what to do with him."

"Sounds like a good plan," I say. "Speaking of plans…"

"We're flying home with the Jersey Devils, aren't we?" Moss responds in a deadpan voice.

"How'd you guess?" I ask, watching as Fe leaps from Moss's head to his shoulder.

"You're louder than you think. I could hear you from a mile away." He rolls his eyes, but I can see the smile forming on his lips. "But I agree. It's safer to ask for their help than go a different way. Joe says there are more people helping that company and I don't want to take any chances."

"Then it's settled," I say.

"Well, you still need to *ask* them if they'll fly us home," Sinistro reminds me.

I pat him on the head and walk over to where the once-enemies now stand together, chattering in hushed tones. The gargoyles and Jersey Devils act as if there were never any issues between them, which is a good thing since they're certainly more alike than they are different.

"I didn't know you could talk to animals," I say to the large gargoyle leader who stopped us earlier in the evening.

"We're gifted with the ability to talk to *all* beings. It's quite useful—especially when making amends for the greater good," he says.

"That sounds promising. Are you going to look out for each other now instead of fight about silly things like who belongs where?"

He nods. "Indeed. We've got bigger matters at hand."

"I'm happy to hear it." I look over his shoulder at the Jersey Devils and walk toward them. Diana's magic is wearing off now that Joe's taken care of and I'm starting to feel the strain on my magic and the tiredness pulling at my eyes. Maybe the Calamoneris will take us to the diner when we get home. But first, I need to coax my waning magic to communicate with the Jersey Devils.

The large black Jersey Devil we met just yesterday— their leader—greets me with a bow of his head. I bow in response and place a gentle hand on his side. His magic mingles with mine and his familiar raspy voice calls to me.

Hello, Giada. Thank you for saving our son.

"Of course." I whisper the words aloud to help my exhausted magic reach him. "I hate to ask you for yet another favor right now…"

Anything. We're forever in your debt.

"Could you take us and the unicorn back to New Jersey?"

We're headed that way. We can take you back.

"Thank you! We'll be ready soon." I hug the Jersey Devil, patting his neck. He neighs in response, shaking out his mane.

I hurry back over to where everyone's standing around Angie's convertible and say, "The Jersey Devils can give us a ride."

Angie opens the driver's side door and Ooh La La jumps in, barking from the passenger seat. "I only fly private. Besides, I'm just a few blocks from here." She looks to Jodi and nods. "You coming, kid?"

Jodi throws her bag in the back seat and smiles at us, her hands on her hips. "Thank you for inviting me on your adventure. It was fun. But I'm ready to get back to learning how to be a Strega del Malocchio."

I envelop Jodi in a hug and smile. "Thank you for your help, Jodi. I'm so sorry for not trusting you. I shouldn't have doubted you for a second. You taught me a lot about the Streghe del Malocchio. We couldn't have done this without you."

244

"Thank you, Giada. I appreciate it." She looks at me, her face breaking into a grin.

"Keep in touch," Moss adds, hugging Jodi next.

"Oh, I will. I'm going to help Angie explain C&C Medicinals to Madre and everyone else."

"We need to spread the word far and wide. Not just in Olde Yorque, but across the other cities, too," Angie says. "You kids should do the same with the magical communities up here."

Jodi scoots onto the passenger's seat next to Ooh La La and buckles in. Angie sits down behind the wheel and revs the engine. "Stay safe out there. You know where to find me if you need help."

They drive back through the grounds, leaving tire marks in the grass. We watch them until the convertible's taillights are shrouded in darkness and the sounds of Frank Sinatra's crooning voice are murmurs on the wind. Then, we say our goodbyes to the gargoyles and hop onto the Jersey Devils for our flight back home.

16

By the time the Jersey Devils get us all back to Moss's house, it's the middle of the night. Which isn't a bad thing since it means the neighbors won't see a group of giant winged cryptids, a fiery phoenix, and a unicorn standing on the front lawn. The Calamoneris and Pulaskis hurry to greet us outside, all sharing looks of anger and relief.

"The city, Moss?" Mrs. Calamoneri chastises, her arms crossed and shoulders rigid. "You know what you did is dangerous. Especially for you. You could've gotten in serious trouble. You could've gotten hurt." She levels Moss with a significant look that makes him go pale. "You went into the city alone. For *two days*?"

"Not alone," Moss says with a nervous laugh. "Giada and Alessia were there, too. So were Fe and Sinistro. And Mrs. Bhandari!"

"Moss, you know what your mom means," Mr. Calamoneri says. "What you did was irresponsible. Thank goodness you went to Irving."

"It was my fault, Mr. and Mrs. Calamoneri," I explain before Moss gets into too much trouble.

"I don't care whose fault it is," Mr. Calamoneri explains. "We were so worried about you kids. You only texted us twice, *twice*, that you were at the school. We saw that your phone was in the city, but then tracking dropped off. The Pulaskis went and searched all over Port Authority and Penn Station. They asked everyone who worked there if they'd seen you. Your mom and I even went back to Teterboro on the off chance that maybe you left the city and caught a bus there. We're lucky Mrs. Bhandari confirmed you were at Irving as we had no clue where you were, and you wouldn't answer us. That's scary, Moss."

"I'm sorry, Dad. Mom." Moss looks past his parents at the Pulaskis. "I'm sorry, Mr. and Mrs. Pulaski."

Alessia apologizes, too.

"I'm sorry, too," I say. "We shouldn't have fallen off the face of the earth. But we had to find the unicorn. And look! We did!"

"Plus a few more friends," Alessia adds.

The Calamoneris and Pulaskis look beyond us to the unicorn, phoenix, and pack of Jersey Devils. Mrs. Pulaski gasps, covering her mouth with her hand. The unicorn swishes her tail, head tilted as she assesses the new humans in front of her.

"They're nice, it's okay," I say to the creatures. "I promise they're not like Joe."

"Joe?" Mr. Pulaski asks. "Who's Joe?"

I go into a tangent about what happened, Moss and Alessia jumping in to add details I miss. We tell them how at first we believed it was the Streghe del Malocchio because of the bad-luck pennies. And how we met a strega named Angie and traveled down to Olde Yorque, only to discover that they were set up and someone else was behind the whole mess. We explain C&C Medicinals and how they're taking magical creatures—not just the unicorn—and creating medicine. How the whole thing is so much bigger than we realized.

Alessia leads Mrs. and Mr. Pulaski over to the unicorn, and they begin carefully checking for any injuries.

"Oh! And Moss not only used his magic to call on and communicate with creatures. He healed a gargoyle all on his own!" I say. "It was so cool."

Mr. Calamoneri looks at Moss, a smile breaking over his face. "You healed a gargoyle, Moss? On your own?"

Moss fidgets with his backpack straps, heat creeping into his cheeks. "Well, Fe helped a ton. But yeah."

"You were incredible, Moss." I beam, putting a hand on his shoulder.

"I'm not gonna lie. After yesterday and today, I'm beyond worn out and my stomach's still terrible. I'm glad we're home so I can get some real rest." He wipes away the sweat from his brow and continues, "Obviously, I still have Crohn's and that's fine. We need to find the treatment plan that works for me, but I don't feel as hopeless about doing that. Being out in the world, working in the field, I think it relit the fire under my magic. You were right, Dad, about changing things up. I used some therapy techniques, like breathing exercises, to help me focus when I started to second-guess myself. I respected my limits and stopped to take breaks when I needed to. It was better than practicing at home. Helping that gargoyle and everything else felt good. I need to start my apprenticeship again. Maybe take it a day at a time."

Mrs. and Mr. Calamoneri exchange a look of excitement before wrapping Moss in a hug. "Of course. We're so proud of you," Mr. Calamoneri says.

"And we'll take it day by day. Just like you want," Mrs. Calamoneri adds.

"What're we gonna do about this organization?" I ask. "We need to let other streghe know what's happening. Angie's gonna talk to the Streghe del Malocchio, but we need to tell everyone else." I throw my hands in the air, already tired at just the thought. "Madonna mia. That's *a lot* of people. I'd have to travel all over the world."

Mrs. Calamoneri looks at me, her eyes alight with an idea. "Well, maybe you can."

"What do you mean?" I furrow my brow.

"I'm leaving on my tour in the next couple weeks. It'll take me everywhere. All over the world. You could come with me."

I blink at her. Travel? All over the world? Excitement builds in my chest. Traveling the world would be cool. But there's just one thing in the way. "What about my apprenticeship? I'm supposed to be working with Mr. Calamoneri for the year. My mamma and papa already bent the rules for me to become a magical vet. I don't think they'd let me skip out on my apprenticeship."

"I'll talk to them. There are magical vets everywhere, Giada. You could continue your training."

"What do you think, Sinistro?" I crouch down, scratching behind his ears. "Are you up for a worldwide adventure?"

"As long as we're not flying on gryphons or Jersey Devils or any other beasts who might drop me into the ocean."

"I'm pretty sure this is a planes-only experience," I laugh.

Sinistro looks satisfied with that answer, and I stand up, nodding at Mrs. Calamoneri. "We'll have a lot of work to do. Who knows if anyone'll believe us."

"I don't know if you should worry about that." Mrs. Calamoneri grins. "You're a convincing young lady."

"Looks like we're back to being pen pals," Moss says.

"Better start practicing your penmanship now. Some of your letters look like they were written by a cockatrice."

"Maybe we should switch to email." Moss laughs and I look at Alessia and the Pulaskis fawning over the unicorn, at the phoenix sitting regally on top of the trash can by the end of the driveway, and the pack of Jersey Devils digging holes into the Calamoneris' perfectly green lawn with their hooves.

I pick up Sinistro and kiss him on the head. Fear wiggles its way into my belly, but I square my shoulders. "We can do this, Sinistro."

"I go where you go," he says, butting his head against mine.

But we won't be alone. Angie and Jodi are going to talk to the Streghe del Malocchio. Alessia is honing her soul magic and will be able to share her spells. Moss is going back to his apprenticeship and can do research.

I'm not going to let people like Joe or C&C Medicinals scare me.

I saved my brother.

I saved a unicorn.

Now I'm going to save all the magical creatures.

They don't know who they're dealing with.

★ ★ ★ ★ ★

ACKNOWLEDGMENTS

There are so many people to thank for this book as it was a true labor of love. First, I want to give a huge thanks to my editor, Meghan McCullough. You're a dream to work with and have pushed me to make this book what it is. I appreciate all your wisdom. To my lovely readers, Jessie Maimone, Carla DeSantis, and Sossity Chiricuzio—your guidance was so crucial to this story. Also, a big shoutout to my brother-in-law, Garrett Lynch, who gave me insight into living with Crohn's. Crohn's is different for every person and learning more about your experience was invaluable. Thank you to Bess Braswell, Brittany Mitchell, Pam Osti, Kamille Carreras Pereira, and the entire Inkyard family for continuing to love Giada so much. And to Devin Elle Kurtz, Jessica Molina, and Alexandra Niit for the gorgeous, gorgeous cover.

I'm also so grateful for CAKE and their infinite magic. Dhonielle, you're beyond incredible—you inspire me every day and I'm lucky to know you. To the amazing Clay Morrell, who is so kind and amazing. And everyone at CAKE who has shaped Giada and her story: Carlyn Greenwald, Haneen Oriqat, Sasha Nanua, Sarena Nanua, Shelly Romero—you're all magical, terrific people.

To the whole New Leaf Literary team, especially Suzie Townsend, Sophia M. Ramos, Olivia Coleman, Jo Volpe, and Jenniea Carter. You all had a huge hand in bringing Giada into the world and are fantastic, patient, and actual superheroes.

To my husband, Dan, who helps me stay focused, suggests fun magical creatures to include, and nudges me to write even when I may not want to. I couldn't do any of this without you and I love you so much. To my dad and sisters, as always, for cheering me on and getting excited whenever I tell them about "book stuff." To Doom, Fester, and AJ—my sweet babies that I wish I could talk to like Giada does with Sinistro. And to my terrific friends Melinda Newman and Danni Aubin for always reminding me why I love to write.

And, finally, to you. Thank you for reading Giada's story. I'm so thrilled that you decided to pick up this book and read it. I hope she has inspired you to discover the magic in your life and to go after your dreams.